The quiet before the storm . . .

Molly stared up and saw all she would ever need in Patrick's eyes.

"When you were tending the fire, I was watching you," she whispered. "I fantasized that you were making love to me here on this sheepskin rug."

She saw the fire in his eyes, felt her own heartbeat answer. The waiting was heated, full, and she knew that his control would break soon.

"Was it a good fantasy?" he asked in a husky voice filled with loving.

"Yes," she whispered, reaching her fingers to touch the dark patch of hair on his chest.

"This will be better," he promised as he bent to take her lips with his.

VANESSA GRANT started writing her first romance at the age of twelve and hasn't forgotten the
excitement of having a love story come to life on paper. After spending four years refitting the forty-six-
foot yacht they live on, she and her husband, Brian,
and their teenage son set sail south to Mexico along
the North American West Coast. Vanessa divides her
time between her writing, sailing and exploring the
harbors of the Pacific Coast. She often writes her love
stories on her portable computer while anchored in
remote inlets. Vanessa says, "I believe in love and
in happy endings."

Books by Vanessa Grant

HARLEQUIN PRESENTS
1264—WILD PASSAGE
1289—TAKING CHANCES
1322—SO MUCH FOR DREAMS
1386—ONE SECRET TOO MANY
1426—THE TOUCH OF LOVE
1490—ANGELA'S AFFAIR

HARLEQUIN ROMANCE
2888—THE CHAUVINIST

VANESSA GRANT

With Strings Attached

Harlequin Books

TORONTO • NEW YORK • LONDON
AMSTERDAM • PARIS • SYDNEY • HAMBURG
STOCKHOLM • ATHENS • TOKYO • MILAN
MADRID • WARSAW • BUDAPEST • AUCKLAND

This story is for Mary
who reads them first

Harlequin Presents first edition February 1993
ISBN 0-373-11528-8

Original hardcover edition published in 1991
by Mills & Boon Limited

WITH STRINGS ATTACHED

CHAPTER ONE

"HAPPY birthday, Molly. The cabin's yours, but get out there right away. I've left Trouble with food for a day or two, that's all..."

Pack up at a moment's notice? Drive three thousand miles in a tearing hurry to rescue a cat! No one but Saul would have the nerve to demand such a crazy favor. No one but Molly would be gullible enough to agree.

"A birthday present," Saul had announced, his voice quick and persuasive on the telephone. Impossible to resist his enthusiasm as he rushed through instructions. "Get to the lawyer today and sign the papers—I've sent them express. Then pack."

Molly remembered every one of the five times her father had marked her birthday with extravagant gifts. Gifts, growled Aunt Carla, instead of apologies for the other times when he had simply forgotten.

He had telephoned the day after her twenty-sixth birthday. From New York, he said rapidly, although the last she heard he had been somewhere on Canada's west coast, deep in preparation for his September showing in Paris.

Sitting in her Ottawa apartment, Molly had closed her greenish-blue eyes and listened to his voice, had felt pleasure sweep over her. She hadn't been expecting a birthday call, certainly not a present. She had learned years ago that anticipation too often led to disappointment. She knew her father loved her, knew it was not realistic to expect a great artist to have everyday virtues. Enough that Aunt Carla and Uncle Gordon had invited her to dinner at their apartment in Toronto; that Thomas, the man she had been dating lately, had brought flowers.

Incredible that Saul should call, beyond belief that he should casually—over the telephone—tell her he was giving her a home, a place of her own. A dream.

It had taken Molly six days of driving, sleeping in rest areas and economy motels, to reach the Pacific Coast. Driving forever, it seemed, but finally the coast had come. Vancouver. The water. The ferry. Journey's end. Soon.

Sitting in her gold van on the car deck of the ferry, Molly finger-combed her shoulder-length black curls and waited for the ramp to go down on Vancouver Island.

An adventure.

She remembered other adventures, excitement tumbling into worry and disaster. Aunt Carla could be right in her assessment of Saul's latest crazy request. One telephone call from her father and Molly's life was turning upside down. Nothing new in that. Her earliest memory was of Saul standing in the middle of a rented studio somewhere, waving a sable paintbrush and announcing that Paris would be a good place to live. For a while.

Molly thought she must have been about five years old that day, all wide eyes and black, curly hair. She knew she was seven when they went to Athens. Eight in London. Eleven in Mexico City. Twelve in Montreal, where it all stopped.

In Montreal, Aunt Carla had descended on Saul and bullied him into sending his daughter to a regular school, a regular home—Aunt Carla's.

Thank God for Aunt Carla and Uncle Gordon, thought Molly as she drove her van down the ferry ramp and on to Vancouver Island. Without the stability of Aunt Carla's home, Molly might never have learned that life could be steady. Peaceful. Geographically stable.

So why, after fourteen years of living quietly first in Toronto, then in a shared Ottawa apartment—why was she letting one telephone call from Saul send her driving off into the sunset? Why, when she had vowed that she would never drive off the edge of the world for anyone again?

"Take it slow," Carla had insisted. "Check it all out first."

Sensible, if it were not for the cat Saul had left behind. Carla had suggested the SPCA, but the cat was Molly's responsibility now. It wasn't that she was counting on Saul's gift of a home. She knew about Saul's gifts. Sometimes he took them back, often he failed to pay for them. Molly had given up her share of the apartment in Ottawa, yes, but she could always go back, find another place to live. She had not burned any bridges that couldn't be rebuilt.

Molly knew she must be careful with Saul's castles in the sky. Careful, but not paranoid. Even if the cabin turned out to be a hovel in a swamp, she would enjoy the adventure.

She followed the flow of cars without a clue where she was. Ashore now. Vancouver Island. The city of Nanaimo, yes, but where in Nanaimo? She could find her way around Ottawa and Montreal and Paris, but this was foreign territory, three thousand miles from home, and she was exhausted.

Last night she had stayed at an economy motel on the outskirts of Vancouver, had spent the night listening to a screaming battle in the next unit. When dawn came, she had packed up and gone for breakfast at an all-night restaurant, then found a drive-in tourist information center. She needed information on how to find Gabriola Island and Saul's cabin.

Her cabin now.

She had tried to sleep on the ferry, but there had been a rough chop and Molly had felt vaguely nauseated all the way from the mainland to Vancouver Island. Where was Saul now? Why could he not have waited? Met her?

Six days' driving, and if Saul had not been in such a crazy rush he would have waited for her before he took off for his mysterious destination. Or given her directions. Molly laughed, knowing how impossible that was, how typical the whole thing was of her father. Who else but a crazy artist would tell her to come, urgently, then totally neglect to give a few basic instructions? "Your house now, Molly, but look after the cat. I've got to leave her alone, so please come right away..."

Molly swung the steering wheel to the left and followed a green car through a controlled intersection. Had she just turned on to the Trans-Canada highway? These British Columbians had a nerve, calling it the Trans-Canada highway after interrupting it for a ferry crossing of Georgia Strait. Where the devil *were* the signs? Could you turn off Route One to that other ferry? Or— Gabriola Island. It must be an Indian name. Or was it Spanish? Gabriola. Yes, Spanish.

She knew so little about it. A gulf island nestled against Vancouver Island. Ferry service to Nanaimo. Mild climate. Romantic. Beautiful, Saul had said, but Saul could see beauty in anything. Her home. How could she say no when Saul suddenly offered her a home of her own? And a cat, for crying out loud, when she knew nothing about cats. Trust Saul to call it a gift, then add that business about the cat, making it impossible for Molly to delay coming.

A cat named Trouble. Molly's lips twitched as she drove through the sudden congestion of Nanaimo's downtown area. Aunt Carla had been full of warnings and doom, but the thought of a cat named *Trouble* had made the whole thing seem more like a story out of one of Molly's children's books.

Aunt Carla, always so calm and cool, had turned wild when Molly told her about the house. "You know what he's like—the neighbors are about to lynch him, or the place is mortgaged and the bank's about to foreclose. Or it's built on a bog and sinking. Molly, it's a trap!"

Saul Natham had been a charmer from his infancy, but Carla had memories of more than once when her elder brother had left her in the middle of a mess, and himself miraculously free of trouble. Saul Natham was trouble. Always had been. He was also an incredibly talented artist, and Molly's father. If he wanted to leave her a house and a troublesome cat, Molly knew she simply had to accept. Carefully.

For all her reservations, she could not resist the growing excitement. Her own home, a log cabin among the trees, within walking distance of the wild Pacific Ocean. A place where she could spread out her easel and Alex's latest manuscript. No downstairs neighbors to complain about the smell of her paints. No landlord to raise the rent.

A place in the country. She had no idea why it fascinated her so, knew it was crazy to yearn for the open countryside. Molly Natham, who had never lived in a city with a population of less than half a million! She had no clear picture of life in the open, only a hazy fantasy. Quite probably, she would suffer cabin fever within twenty-four hours.

Saul's voice over the telephone had painted a magical picture. No directions, but enchantment promised if she ever found the place. Molly had fantasized herself taking root on Saul's island with the strange name. Gabriola. Perhaps she would stay forever. The island children would tiptoe past and whisper about the strange old maid who painted dinosaur pictures. Molly would go for walks, smell the evergreens and watch the deer. Her own place. Not a condo eleven storeys above the ground, as she had been thinking of buying lately, but a real cabin with real land and real trees, her own plot of dirt.

She had not told anyone how the dream excited her, not Aunt Carla or Uncle Gordon. Certainly not Thomas, who had stared at her with accusation when she'd announced she was leaving. She had felt uncomfortable at the look in Thomas's eyes, knowing he would never be more than a friend to her.

Probably no man would. She was as restrained in her relations as her father was extravagant. She simply did not have Saul's depth of feeling.

Better that way. Saul was an extraordinary artist, but his life was all tragedy and ecstasy and crises. Molly needed tranquillity, which let out greatness and falling in love.

"*Gabriola Ferry.*" Molly saw the sign too late. She was in the wrong lane and the traffic was too heavy to change. She turned right at the intersection, meaning to double around, but found herself driving uphill heaven knew where, with no chance of doubling back. She kept trying to turn right and right again, to retrace her steps, but in fact it took her fifteen minutes to find her way back to the street with the sign.

Trouble. Six days' driving. Eight days since Saul had called. Had he left the poor cat alone? Surely he would have found a neighbor to look after it? Were there neighbors? The cat named Trouble had haunted Molly ever since Saul called. She had thrown her things into the van in a fury of activity. She had called the movers to take the extra boxes to Aunt Carla's and Uncle Gordon's for storage; then made a flying trip to the bank for cash, to the post office to arrange for her mail to be redirected to Aunt Carla.

Rushing, worried about a cat she had never met. Trouble was the cat's name, but if Aunt Carla had her way Trouble would be Saul's first name, too. There! The ferry sign. Gabriola.

She paid her fare and asked for a copy of the schedule. Then she drove ahead into lane number one as she was instructed. She parked her van at the front of the empty lane and studied the schedule. The next ferry would not leave for forty minutes. Commuter tickets. Next time, she would buy a book of them. The thought gave her a pleasing feeling of belonging.

Would hers be the only vehicle on the ferry?

Molly locked her van and went into the small waiting room near the ferry ramp. Empty. Obviously midafternoon was a quiet time for the ferry. She studied the bulletin board, intrigued.

"Jill-of-all-trades looking for work on Gabriola: milking goats, chopping wood, tending babies..." "Two-ton truck for sale, good work truck with rough body..." "Zen meditation classes..." "Poetry readings..." "Sunday dinner special at a Gabriola pub..." "Student needs ride to 8:00 a.m. ferry from Silva Bay."

Molly prowled along the bulletin board, reading about apples and fresh honey for sale. A Saturday meeting for islanders to protest about a proposed industrial plant. A ratepayers meeting to discuss applications for zoning changes. A play to be performed at the community hall, depicting the settling and development of the Gulf Islands.

She had come a long way. All the way from Ottawa to an island small enough to put up community notice boards. Molly left the waiting room, her lips curved in a smile. She might even go to that play herself.

There was another vehicle behind hers now, a white classic Corvette with its convertible top down. Molly felt increasingly aware of the man at the wheel as she crossed the pavement toward her own vehicle. Just the two of them, alone in the ferry lineup. Would she eventually come to know who he was? Would she learn all the islanders by name? How many were there?

Should she smile at him? Say hello? Or simply lift her hand in a casual greeting? Or nothing? Was it true that country people were friendlier? Fantasy, to think she would come to belong. She looked out over the water, wondered which way the ferry came and whether that island across the harbor was her new home.

Home? Or a temporary residence? Somewhere in all this there had to be a catch; perhaps even the potential for disaster that was so often entangled with Saul's impulses.

It was a gorgeous car, sleek and white and impractical, but it was the man who made her feel flustered— too conscious of herself and restlessly aware of him. He had dark hair, perhaps pure black like her own. His curls had escaped to determined freedom across one side of his forehead. A moustache, black and strong above his upper lip. Sexy, she thought, then glanced away quickly. His face remained clearly focused in her mind. Tanned skin, or was it naturally dark? Eyes—dark brown? Or black?

Unbelievable. She had only glanced at him, more at the car really, but her mind held the image. Well, she was an artist, wasn't she? Yes, but she did not normally wander around taking mental snapshots of intriguing men. If she were a portrait painter, he would make a good subject. Arresting face, dark and strong and...well, sensual. Or was it the mental association of the open sports car that gave that impact?

She felt his eyes touching her as she tried to jam the ignition key into the door lock. She realized her mistake and found the right key, then tried to insert it upside down.

"On holiday?"

His voice was deep, filled with pleasant harmonics. She looked up, straight into his eyes. Too close. Twenty feet away, but it seemed that he was staring directly into her mind. She felt a flush rising and her usually quiet voice came out in a sharp challenge.

"What makes you think that?"

Friendly place, Saul had said. Not nosy, which would be a drag, but people were easy to talk to. The man in the Corvette was amused, although it was crazy to think she could see laughter in a pair of black eyes twenty feet away.

"Your license plates," he explained reasonably. "Ontario plates. And you locked your car, which isn't exactly island style."

Island style. In the city, she would have frozen him with one cold glance, but she had no idea what you said to a fellow islander. She remembered the easy informality of the bulletin board and felt awkwardly out of place.

She frowned and tried to pretend he wasn't watching her, but could not help feeling that he liked what he saw.

He would be tall. His shoulders were broad under that soft maroon sweater. Expensive sweater, with an immaculate shirt collar rising neatly above the V-neck, a tie that echoed the sweater. He had good taste, or someone who picked his clothes did. Wife? Girlfriend? His lips were curved slightly, waiting to smile. The edge of the off-white collar contrasted against the dark, tanned flesh of his neck. If her fingers brushed along the side of his neck, would his skin feel cool? Or hot and dry? Would it—stop it!

"Are you staying on the island?" he asked.

Ridiculous to feel goose bumps along her midriff from the sound of a voice. "Yes," she muttered as the key finally turned in the lock of the door.

She was *not* going to succumb to the strange impulse to stand here talking to him, asking if he was an islander, why he was driving around in midafternoon when he looked like a man who was a successful something. Lawyer, perhaps. Or accountant. Doctor. Not run-of-the-mill, whatever he was. Impulsive, she decided, although he would keep it under a stern leash. She swung open the door to her van and nodded in his general direction with deliberate breeziness. Then she twisted her way behind the steering wheel and slammed the door. She felt like a fool.

She had an uncanny conviction that the stranger knew exactly how peculiar he made her feel.

When the van stayed on South Road at the Gabriola post office turn, Patrick McNaughton canceled his own left turn signal and followed.

As if he had no choice.

He sucked in a deep breath and forced his grip on the steering wheel to relax. What the hell had got into him? Those images playing on his mind from the instant when he first saw her. A woman, a stranger, walking toward him. She had curly black hair that would twist and cling to a man's fingers when he caressed it. He had watched and the images had exploded.

For all he knew, she had a brain the size of a peanut under that wonderful hair. Even if she had the intelligence to carry on a rational conversation, she had shown no desire to do so. Not with him. She had not looked directly at him, just that one startled flash of soft eyes when he'd spoken to her back on the Nanaimo side. Obviously a city girl, astounded at his casual informality.

How many years since he had spoken to a strange woman, fully intending to pursue her? In recent years his affairs had been careful, safe, and not at all frequent. Today, for example, the man-woman game had been the last thing on his mind. He had been deep in the problem of the Haddleson top-down design, oblivious to the world. He could not remember giving his commuter pass to the woman in the BC Ferries ticket booth. Or had it been a man? Patrick had been too deep in thought to notice. He did remember pulling away from the booth, though, driving into the ferry lineup; except that in midafternoon it wasn't a lineup at all. Just one other vehicle.

Patrick had braked and turned off the engine, snapped open his briefcase and pulled out his notebook computer. "Haddleson." The little green light above the keys had blinked as the file came on-screen. "Outline. Level one: input-output criteria. Level two..."

His eyes had moved away from the screen, caught by some movement in his peripheral vision while his fingers kept typing.

Then his hands had stilled.

She was walking toward him, must have come out of the waiting room. Immaculate blue denim jeans and medium-heeled sandals. A green collar under her bulky, rust-colored sweater. She was tall enough to make those long, slender legs seem right. Perfect, in fact. She had a loose, long-limbed way of moving that made him think of innocent sensuality. Her hips were slender, but the movement of her walk encouraged her sweater to pull against a woman's voluptuous breasts.

He had felt the hard rhythm of his own pulse echoing through his body. Something about the way she walked. Something...

For a man who sometimes had problems remembering the names and faces of people he'd just met, Patrick was left with an impossibly vivid picture of *her* face. Her features were drawn a little too sharply. His mother would say that she needed feeding. Big, big eyes that caught at something inside him. Patrick thought she worked too hard, too intensely. She needed laughter. He wanted to give it to her.

She was not beautiful, although it would be impossible to feel the pull of any other woman if she were in the room. Something in her eyes. He wished he were closer, could see better.

Eyes. Her eyes. Not brown. Not blue either. He had to know...

Was he really following a total stranger to learn the color of her eyes? The van slowed abruptly and Patrick shifted down into second gear. She was driving a little erratically, a stranger to the awkward curves that made speeding both dangerous and uncomfortable on Gabriola. Ontario plates. He had memorized the numbers, had memorized the woman, seeing the echo of her face and remembering her voice all through the twenty-minute ferry ride. Her face, when all he could actually *see* was the dark silhouette of her hair through the van's windows on the ferry. Her voice, when she had said a total of six words to him. "What makes you think that?" and "Yes."

His mind dissolved into a graphic fantasy. Yes. Would she say yes if he kissed those lips gently, exploring the softness, searching for her surrender?

More likely she would slap his face.

He had spent the entire ferry ride to Gabriola trying to concentrate on the screen of the notebook computer, fighting the magnetic pull that drew his eyes to the silhouette in the window of the van in front of him. Impossible, it turned out, and in the end he had actually started a new file and typed into it what he knew about her.

She came from back East. Ontario, but where? Toronto, perhaps? Age, mid-twenties. Height, five feet seven or eight. He tried to put that into centimetres but got lost in deciding that the top of her head would come somewhere around his lips. He would bend and bury his face in the soft riot of her curls. She had a walk that would make a fortune for a dancer. A husky, low voice that sent crawling awareness along Patrick's veins. What would her laughter do to his pulse? Would her eyes soften with loving? He had not seen their color, but the message had been very plain. She had no interest in the searing awareness she had stirred in Patrick McNaughton.

But she had felt it. He remembered that electric feeling of awareness, her hand fumbling with the keys to her van.

Five minutes after the ferry left the Nanaimo dock, Patrick had watched her get out of her van and walk forward to stand at the rail. After a few minutes in the cool ocean wind, she had gone inside to the passenger lounge. Patrick had wanted to go with her, to shelter her from the cold with his arms.

He had forced himself not to follow her. She obviously did not want him at her side, had carefully avoided looking at his car. He was certain, though, that she was every bit as aware of him as he was of her. He would follow on the Gabriola side, until he found out the color of her eyes and where she was staying. She wasn't a woman to be picked up by a stranger, but if he met her in the normal way it might be different. Uneasily, he realized that with all the new people moving on to the island recently, he might not know the people she was staying with.

She might have come to visit a girlfriend or some distant cousin. She might be staying at one of the bed and breakfasts, a tourist on holiday. He would find out.

She might be married.

He suspected that he would wake up some time this evening and feel like a fool. Following a woman, for heaven's sake! Those few seconds of watching her in motion kept playing again and again in his mind. She was lean, yet soft woman. His blood kept pounding. He felt hot, dizzy, as if his fingers had brushed the soft, warm curves of her femininity.

Abruptly, her van pulled off on to a wide gravel shoulder. Patrick was past before he could brake, his eyes echoing with a glimpse of her face turned to watch as he drove past. Resentment or anger in her eyes.

He realized that his hands and his feet were making motions, gearing down, braking. Stop. Go back. Ask her...

Ask her *what* for God's sake?

He jammed his foot to the floor. The Corvette took off along South Road with a whine of power.

It was probably that damned book his sister Sarah had been reading lately. Just last night she had been telling him he was overdue for his thirties crisis.

"You see, Pat, you've built your little empire—well, your biggish empire."

"A big frog in a little pond," he'd countered lightly. "Vancouver Island isn't the world."

"No, but—listen to me, Pat! You've been devoting all your time to success. What about falling in love? Having children of your own? It's going to hit you one of these days! Time's running out for you, and you'll go down like a ton of bricks, because you're ripe for realizing how much you're missing."

With Sarah's theory ringing in his ears, Patrick followed South Road around the bottom of the island until it became North Road, then he turned off and drove up the hill, past the McNaughton farm and on to the small subdivision of five-acre parcels his father had developed twenty years ago. Sarah and her brothers had each fallen heir to one of the parcels on their twenty-first birthdays. Sarah and her husband had built a bed and breakfast on their land. Patrick had built the cedar home that was really too big for him, but he could not imagine living anywhere else now. David, their older brother, had sold his acreage and put the money into the family farm that he now managed.

Funny tricks the subconscious played. Sarah's self-help book, her words echoing in Patrick's mind. To be honest, he had caught himself now and then lately feeling an emptiness in the moments between jobs. He needed a change, something new, had even considered saying yes to the committee that had approached him about running for a seat in the British Columbia legislature.

New frontiers, that was what he needed.

He had always thought he would marry eventually, when the time and the woman were right. But the years had passed and he had never met a woman he wanted to share his home with. He would have liked children, but the thought of opening his walls to the wrong woman was frightening.

The woman in the van, waking in his bed with her eyes sleepy and filled with love.

A symbol. She would be married, her own life, even her own children. Something in her walk had caught his imagination, that was all. A signal, perhaps, that he should think about finding someone to share his home with, his life.

No hurry, he decided, shaking off the stranger's spell. He turned into his own driveway, more comfortable now that the crazy compulsion to pursue the strange woman had passed. He parked beside the two-story cedarwood home nestled under the evergreens. A wisp of smoke crawled out of the chimney. He had banked the wood fire down this morning. After a surprisingly cool night, the April sun had risen to warm the house, beating in through the skylights in his cathedral ceiling.

Patrick froze as a strange sound echoed through the clearing. A second later, it resonated again, a grating noise invading the quiet. How many times lately had he woken in the middle of the night to that strange cross between a rustle and a twang? Too often!

He dropped the briefcase on the veranda and ran around to the back of the house. Patrick liked to eat back here in the sun room, enjoying the sight of the pond where the deer came at sunset, the smell of the dogwood blossoms. Every spring he took the glass windows off and replaced them with screens, only this year Saul Natham had bought the property next door, had moved in and almost immediately added that damned cat to his household!

There she was, attacking the sun room again!

"Get off there!" His voice rang angrily through the trees and the cat froze. "Yes, you damned ball of fluff! I mean you! Get the hell off my screen!"

She was halfway up the side of the building, a streaky black and white mass of soft fur, plastered flat against the screen, claws curling through the fine fabric of the mesh. Patrick could see the scars from the path she had taken on her way up.

He turned away. He needed the ladder. What the hell could a man say to an animal who was probably only looking for a warm place to curl up? He would peel the bloody cat off his screen again, then he would feed it, although last time it had refused to touch his offerings.

This time, Patrick wasn't going to replace the bloody screen until Saul Natham turned up from wherever he had gone. Natham was going to get a surprise when he returned. So far, Patrick and Natham had shared a few lazy conversations, nothing more. Enough talk for Patrick to know the artist was both entertaining and eccentric. An interesting neighbor, and thankfully his faults did not include sending loud heavy music echoing through the trees.

Now, though, Patrick was determined to make the irresponsible artist take his damned cat and look after it

properly if it was the last thing he did! What kind of a
man adopted a cat from the SPCA, then went off and
left the thing to fend for itself? The poor beast had been
howling for days after Natham had disappeared, then it
had decided to attach itself to Patrick's house.

To his house, but not to Patrick himself. The cat had
accepted the odd offering of food, but hadn't consented
to come inside when Patrick was home. That hadn't
stopped her from trying to *break* in when the place was
empty, tearing up window screens and once getting stuck
in the chimney and emerging black and wild-eyed.
Patrick had angry red scratches on his forearms from
his battle to bathe the sooty cat after that fiasco!

The cat didn't want a new home, she wanted Saul
Natham back. God knew what it was about the aging
artist next door, but the female population of the world
was determined that he was irresistible—including the
cat currently stuck to Patrick's sun-room screen. How
else could you explain the parade of long-legged women
next door? Patrick had seen at least three different
blondes draped over Natham as they walked that path
through the back of Pat's property. But a cat, for
heaven's sake! Surely a feline should have sense enough
to abandon such an erratic personality and find herself
a dependable master!

When Saul Natham got back...

CHAPTER TWO

DAMN Saul! He had talked as if the island were too small for Molly to lose her way. Lot three, McNaughton Road, he had told her. No other directions.

After Molly had shaken the disturbing man in the sports car, she had driven all over Gabriola Island, looking for McNaughton Road and finding everything but. Had the man really been following her? A golf course. A community center. Houses scattered lightly, half hidden in the trees. Signs for everything from Degnen Bay to Drumbeg Provincial Park, but no McNaughton road.

Peterson Road. Silva Bay Road. Of course he had not been following. Just a coincidence—whoops! That sign said *North* Road, not South. She frowned and followed the winding pavement past a miniature shopping center, a medical clinic nested in the trees, and a school.

She ended up back at the ferry terminal.

She did the whole circuit again, looking for a turn-off she might have missed. Twice around the island and she learned that the evergreens growing on the roadsides reached to touch each other high over the road, that the ocean could be glimpsed in sudden spectacular explosions here and there along the route. South Road ran for thirteen kilometres before it turned into North Road. North Road ran the thirteen kilometres back to the ferry terminal.

"Welcome to Gabriola," the sign said. It was a map of sorts, painted on a large board where anyone driving on to the island would see it. McNaughton Road was not named on the map.

While she stared at the painted map, a school bus backed down the road to the ferry ramp. She realized that she had the island turned around in her mind. Somehow she had thought west was that way, but——

The ferry docked again, this time ejecting thirty or so teenagers who ran noisily on to a waiting school bus. The bus roared away slowly, then the cars streamed off the ferry. Useful facts she was collecting about this island. The high school students went to Nanaimo for their schooling, came back just after four in the afternoon. There was a post office, a pub, at least three restaurants and two gas stations. A medical clinic.

No McNaughton Road.

Once the traffic from the ferry had thinned out, Molly started on another circuit, intending to explore some of those side roads. Soon it would be time to stop and ask, but it would be a small victory if she could find Saul's cabin for herself, without help from the locals.

She turned left and lost herself in a network of interconnecting side streets. When the pavement changed to gravel, Molly turned back and took a break in a provincial park nestled on the shore. She walked on the beach, through the trees, breathing the salt air and enjoying herself, realizing that she was never going to find Saul's cabin without asking the way.

She drove to the neighborhood pub near the ferry terminal. It was noisy, friendly, and when the waitress said, "Dinner? Or just a drink?" Molly realized that she *was* hungry. She ordered a hamburger that turned out to be massive, then ate while she watched the regulars enjoying a baseball game on television. This time, when she set off again, she had directions.

"Follow North Road past Peterson. First turn right after Peterson, follow the road up the hill. Then right again past the McNaughton Farm. There are only six lots up there. You'll find the one you want easy enough.''

Easy enough, if Saul had thought to give instructions. Molly had the papers from the lawyer with her, and the echo of the command from Saul. She had a house and a cat and she had wasted several enjoyable hours wandering this island. Soon it would be dark.

Where was the man in the white sports car? For a while there, she'd had the breathless conviction that she would never escape him. Driving, knowing he was following her, she had succumbed to the weirdest fantasies, straight out of some romantic, far-out novel. Thank God he had driven on when she'd pulled off the road! If he had stopped and walked back to her...

Molly forgot the black-eyed man as she drove up the hill past the farm. Those open fields, the cows grazing. Pastoral, glimpses of little meadows winding through the forest. A bed-and-breakfast sign, then another driveway winding into the trees, a carved board announcing lot two and the name ''McNaughton.'' The instructions were working!

McNaughton of McNaughton Road and McNaughton farm, she decided with a grin. Undoubtedly the McNaughtons had lived here for generations, perhaps emigrated directly from the old country to build their family empire here on Gabriola Island.

Odd that her wandering father should buy a property in the midst of all this obvious stability.

The next drive must be hers, although there was no sign, just a winding gravel drive that badly needed smoothing. Molly jolted along, the van scraping against the branches of overgrown fir trees on one side, dragging bottom briefly on one rutted section. If there was a house up here, she couldn't see it. How big *was* five acres? Was she actually on lot three? She followed the winding detour around a big, old tree.

There it was.

The cabin might well have been built from logs cut down from this very property. Cut and chinked and painstakingly assembled into a home. A small home, but there must be a loft. The upper part had a little balcony that overhung the porch, supported by big logs. Molly had never been in a house with an open loft, but the thought of standing up there at an easel, looking down into her home, out over *her* land...

She blinked away moisture at her eyes. Had Saul known how she yearned for a real home? She was twenty-six years old, and finally her father was making a home for her. She left the door to the van swinging wide, her attention on the cabin, the cedar trees with their branches hanging down over the cedar shake roof.

Hers.

She turned, her eyes sweeping a circle from the cabin, over the clearing and the drive. The sun was low in the sky, reddish light slanting through those trees. That must be west. She swung further, saw the beginning of a narrow path that led into the trees, a stand of thin young trees behind the cabin, then the cedars. She had to learn the names of all these other trees.

No neighbors in sight. Five acres, Saul had said, but the lawyer's papers had described it as just over two hectares. Metric or imperial, it was enough land for total privacy.

All hers.

What would a tyrannosaurus rex look like, wandering out from those trees? She giggled, thinking of the man in the sports car. He would think she was a nut if he could overhear her thoughts. Dinosaurs and fantasies. Whoever he was, he would never know how fanciful she could be. No one would, because Molly knew how to keep her fantasies in their proper place.

Tomorrow. She would wander outside in the morning light with her sketching pad. Rex and Bronty and Terry. A smile curved on her lips as she thought of a whole new series of dinosaur paintings. Impossibly nice that her silly prehistoric fantasies were selling so well in the gallery. Of course, she had to get the sketches done for the new book, that was her real bread and butter, and there was no way she could use a rural setting for the book illustrations. It was completely a city tale. But in her spare time——

Were there bears out in those trees? She had better get inside before dark. She wanted lights on when night came. What if the place didn't have electricity? Molly scanned the cabin, looking for wires, evidence of electricity and telephone. Nothing.

The front door was locked. Of course it was locked. She hadn't thought of keys at all.

She stepped back off the porch and walked around the cabin. She picked her way through a thick growth of leafy, dark green plants; around a barrel placed to catch rainwater from the eaves. What about running water? Molly peered into the barrel. Half full. A layer of dust over the water. Some kind of insect crawling across the surface.

There was a grove of cedar trees at the back of the cabin, the ground beneath carpeted with cedar needles gone a warm brown color. The back door was locked, but she wasn't too disappointed. Saul was notoriously bad about security. She would find a window open somewhere. In Paris they'd had their apartment ransacked twice, everything gone, because Saul perpetually forgot to lock up.

Having signed the transfer with the lawyer and made the birthday phone call, he would have forgotten all about the house and the cat and every detail associated with them. He certainly would not waste time worrying about keys, but surely one of these windows would open?

The window beside the door didn't budge when Molly tried to push upward on the bottom pane. More than a week since Saul had phoned. What if the cat had starved? Would she find its body out there in the trees? Could cats fend for themselves in the woods? Would there be mice for the cat to hunt? Birds? She could hear birds in the trees, had seen a little blue songster flitting from one branch to another. She hated to think that the cat would attack a little bird like that, but if it was starving...

Molly circled the cabin again, looking for a dish filled with some kind of dry cat food. Surely Saul had filled the animal's dish with food before he'd gone? Enough food to last a few days. How was she going to get inside? Break a window? Could she slip a credit card between the door and the jamb? Would that really work?

She went back to the van for her purse. She got her VISA card out, decided it might be mutilated by an encounter with the latch and substituted a gas company card. She could always use VISA at the Petro-Canada station, but she couldn't use the gas card at Woodwards.

The card slid in, then encountered something immovable. No matter how much she wiggled and twisted the piece of plastic, nothing happened. The person who built the house had not intended this door to be opened by a little rectangle of plastic. It——

The cat! She could hear it!

She swung around sharply.

The man from the ferry. He was standing at the front of the porch steps. If anything, he was taller than she had guessed. And his hair *was* black, coal black and curly, just as dark as those eyes. She gulped and felt her jaw clench with the tension, but managed to demand, "What are you doing to that cat? Let it go!"

He shifted his grip on the scruff of the cat's neck. The poor thing was probably in pain, being held like that. He took a firmer grip and demanded harshly, "What are *you* doing? Breaking in?" His voice had none of the husky invitation she had heard in it earlier.

The cat made a faint *mewing* sound. Molly took a step toward it, stopped abruptly when those black eyes pinned hers.

"Is that Trouble?" Her voice sounded weak, as if it belonged to a Victorian maiden about to swoon. She gritted her teeth and repeated, "Have you got Trouble there?"

"I would say that you're the one looking for trouble." The cat struggled and he gave it a wary glance, then muttered, "Lady, you'd better stop trying to break in and go find some legal accommodation for yourself."

She gasped. "Legal? I——"

"If you're that hard up, couldn't you sleep in your van?" A muscle jumped in his jaw and Molly shivered.

"We do have police on this island, an RCMP detachment on South Road." The cat's hind legs got a grip on his arm and dug into the sweater he was wearing. "And *you* just stay put!" he growled.

Molly found her voice. "Let go of that poor cat!"

He gave a bark of laughter as his eyes swept over her. "You're going to make me? I'd like to see you try. And this cat doesn't need anybody's sympathy. She's probably the most dangerous creature on Gabriola."

Earlier, when he had been sitting in his sports car, Molly had thought that he looked civilized and sexy. Here, with his clothing rumpled and that black hair tumbling down over his forehead, he looked more dangerous than the bears she had fantasized out there in the bushes.

She was damned if she would be intimidated by a man with dangerous black eyes. She growled, "If that's Trouble, that's my cat."

He snorted. "She's trouble all right." He shook his head abruptly. "Lady, what the hell are you talking about?"

She jammed her hands into her jeans pockets. She knew it was ridiculous to try to look aggressive and dangerous when she was facing down six foot something of hard, lean muscle, but she was not about to give in.

She announced flatly, "You're the one who's trespassing. This isn't your property."

"No," he agreed with dangerous quiet. "Nor yours. It belongs to Saul Natham. Since he's not here, I'm protecting his property rights. That cat's his, too, the bloody monster."

"That's Trouble? It's alive? I was afraid——" How was she going to get Trouble away from him? He was holding it—her—as if he were considering strangulation. Molly moved two steps closer, to the edge of the porch. "It's mine. Let go of it."

Close up, he seemed even larger. Molly was tall herself, but it wasn't just his height. The bulk under that sweater had to be pure muscle. Molly would swear there wasn't an ounce of fat on that lean body. Even the hands holding the poor cat looked hard and strong enough to grab Molly and...

"It's my cat." She did *not* want to think about those hands, about their harsh grip turning gentle and caressing. She repeated doggedly, "My cat. Let it go."

She was close enough now to see that his thumb was stroking the cat's chin, although he still held the scruff of its neck in a deathly grip. His eyes jerked from her to the van with its open door. Then back again. "No one in their right mind would want this cat. Who the hell are you? What are you doing here?"

"The cat's mine. Saul gave it to me."

He looked stunned. "Saul——"

"Yes," she snapped stiffly, not meeting his eyes. Those eyes were too dangerous, catching hers and making her wish his voice would turn warm and friendly again, as it had been the first time she heard it. She tensed her jaw, focused on the cat and repeated, "Yes. Mine. Saul gave it to me."

Abruptly, he dropped the cat. It ran three steps, then turned and looked at the man, then at Molly, with wild eyes.

"Trouble," she whispered. "Here, Trouble. Come here."

The cat fled, disappearing into the trees with a rustle, then nothing. Silence.

"Trouble?" he echoed, staring after the cat. Why did she have the feeling that he was avoiding looking at her now? She pulled her hands out of her pockets, freeing her arms to hug herself. The sun was gone, the sky turned gray and cold.

"The cat's name is Trouble. You'd know that if——"

"Trouble?" His laughter sounded almost bitter. "It would be. And lady, if it's your——"

"My name's Molly. Not *lady*."

"Molly——" He made it sound derisive. His gaze moved from her eyes to her lips, down to her sweater, lingering there before it followed the sweater to the lean length of her long legs. "I assume you're one of Saul's...*friends*?"

She felt the heat crawl up her neck and into her face. She opened her lips to deny, but somehow the words would not come.

He took the three steps up to the porch in two easy strides. "Where's Saul?" He was too close. She could feel his presence, an impact on her senses. A clean male smell, the sound of his breathing, the sensation of anger or frustration held in. He pulled her card out of the door and looked down at it. "Why the credit card stunt? Petro-Canada isn't going to honor this card now, you know."

She grabbed the mutilated card from him. "I suppose not. Do you know where he keeps his spare key?"

His eyes narrowed. "You want me to help you get inside?"

The light was going fast. She met his eyes. "Yes, please. You're the next-door neighbor, aren't you? Mr.— McNaughton?"

He shrugged. "Your knowing my name hardly proves anything."

She licked her lips. "I'm not trying to prove——"

"I'm not about to help you break into a neighbor's house."

She supposed he was right to be suspicious of her. She could easily prove her right to be here, could show him the lawyer's papers and identification in her van. Somehow, she felt unwilling to do either. "I—look, Saul called me last week and demanded I drive out here and rescue his cat, Trouble. And—well, he just forgot to tell me where the key was."

He was staring at her. She shook her hair back, trying to escape that uncomfortable examination he was making of her. He looked disapproving, although his voice was neutral as he demanded quietly, "So you really are one of his women?"

"I'm Molly." If she said she was Saul's daughter, the scorn would leave his eyes. Somehow, that stirred her to an unusual anger. He had no right to judge her and she was damned if she had to explain herself to him. She muttered, "I'm not anybody's *woman*," giving the word the same derogatory tones he had. She could have sworn he looked uncomfortable and she pressed her advantage, adding, ''Are you in the habit of sneering at your neighbor's private life?''

The cleft in his chin deepened as his jaw jutted out. ''No,'' he said abruptly. He pushed back the curly tangle of hair from his forehead. ''Sorry. I was out of line. Put it down to an...an odd day.'' He sounded uncomfortable, but not sorry.

Abruptly, the remaining light faded from the sky and left her neighbor as only a shadow on the horizon. She stared at the darkness and said hurriedly, ''Look, I'm—I'm really not a prowler. I'm here because Saul asked me to come, and—well, you can go back to your place. There's no need——''

''How are you going to get in?''

''That's my problem, isn't it? Not yours.'' She smiled brightly and realized the fake smile was pointless in the dark.

The problem of getting inside Saul's gift was one she hadn't solved. She supposed she would have to break a window. But not until he was gone.

He didn't move. She shrugged and turned away, feeling her back crawl with the awareness of his eyes on her. Damn the man! Maybe if she pretended he wasn't there he would eventually go away. There wasn't enough light to see, but she ran her hands along the top of the door jamb. She came away with dusty-feeling fingers, but no key. Next she tried the upper ledge of the window that looked out on the porch. Nothing there either.

She stepped back and gasped at the hard warmth of a man's body against her buttocks. She gasped, 'You——'' and tried to turn, but his hands were on her shoulders, holding her. Not roughly, but implacably.

His voice was a rumble she could feel all through her body. ''Surely if he invited you, he would have told you how to get in? Or was he going to meet you here?''

"No." She couldn't seem to move. She felt panic crawling along her veins, told herself it was fear making her breathing harsh and shallow. "I—no—let me go!" She was free. She stumbled ahead, away from him, swung around with her hands flat behind her, against the log wall of the cabin.

He was only a shadow, a voice. "A man doesn't invite a woman and leave her facing a locked door."

This man wouldn't. If *he* invited her—no, stop it! she told herself harshly. What *was* it about him that made her feel so vulnerable? And the images! Wild and seductive, impressions of touches and caresses, of holding and nestling close. Of feeling . . . feeling . . .

"You don't know Saul," she whispered desperately. "He's capable of forgetting everything, not least my existence. Would you please get out of my way? Please, so I can look for the key."

"Are you sure there's a key?"

"No, of course I'm not sure. Not with Saul." She moved to the right and he did nothing to stop her. She felt her lungs taking air again.

What was the man doing to her brain? Fantasies in her work were one thing, but wild emotional reactions weren't normally in Molly's dictionary. Was the wildness something that came on only with age? She was Saul's child. It might be in her genes, waiting to spring on her. When had Saul started behaving like the charming weirdo he was now? At birth, she had always assumed.

She wondered what her neighbor's first name was.

"I'll check that for you," his rumbling voice offered as she tried to reach the top of the windows at the side of the cabin.

"No, thanks. If I can't reach it, Saul wouldn't have put it there. He's only an inch taller than I am."

"You've known him a long time?"

"Forever," she answered with a wry humor. It was amusing, really, that he thought she was one of Saul's loves. Obviously, Saul had been living here long enough to allow the neighbors to see a few women coming and going.

She turned around, saw only darkness and knew from some sixth sense that he was gone. She shivered, abruptly aware of how alone she was up here in the darkness of night. Too dark. Too alone now that he had abruptly abandoned her. She would have to go back to that bed and breakfast and see if she could stay the night. Tomorrow, in the light of the day, she would come and find a way inside.

Then she heard his voice, close and low. She jerked and stumbled in the low bushes beside the house. "I— I thought you'd gone. Where are you? What did you say?"

His footsteps, more an impression of movement on the night than a sound. The dark breadth of his body, shadow on shadow. When his hand closed over her arm, she jumped. His fingers slid down to link with hers.

"Come on. I've got the back door open for you."

He drew her gently toward him and she followed, muttering, "Have you got cat's eyes? Can you actually see?"

"Some." He let her hand go, dropped his arm around her shoulders and pulled her against him, warning, "Careful, the ground's uneven here."

She felt herself melting against his body, soaking in his warmth and strength. She stiffened and fought the sensation of belonging, of wanting. He had a frightening magnetism.

"How—how did you get the door open?"

"Penknife. It's not much of a lock. Here, watch that step. The back porch is here."

She stumbled and he caught her closer. For just an instant, she felt the heat of his body close against hers, then she pulled away. "Do you think there's any electric—oh!"

Light flooded everywhere. Too bright—at first she could only blink, then she saw him and it felt like the first time again, that odd sensation of recognition. Nervously, she told herself it was the porch light, and the man was...just a man. "I—I didn't think there was power. No wires. I couldn't see any wires."

The door was standing open. She walked past him, could feel his presence behind her. She saw a switch on a wall and threw it on. More light, anything to dispel the dark feeling of intimacy. "Thank you. I—thanks for helping me get in. I'll be fine now."

Somehow, she had known he would not leave that easily. Did he feel it, too?

The light was soft inside, absorbed by the darkness of the log walls. Beyond the kitchen area, illumination crawled softly into a spacious living-room area, with shadows cast by the flight of stairs going up. She whispered, "I knew there'd be a loft. I knew it." She could not resist the stairs, climbed up slowly, picturing the trees outside although it was too dark to see through the windows.

She stood at the very top, staring into the shadowy loft. There was a sofa on the far side that would make down into a bed. Saul's studio easel, near the rail where the light from the windows would flood onto his canvas. Why had he left his easel behind? No matter. He would be back for it. Meanwhile, she would use it instead of unpacking hers from the van.

A walkway led across the open area above the living room, terminating at a door that must open on to a balcony. Molly moved along it, her hand sliding on the rail. She wanted to stand outside in the darkness, to soak in the feel of her new home.

She gasped at the voice close behind her, spun and he was there, only two steps away. Inside her walls. Awareness tingled along her flesh.

The frown was in his voice. "Why? What do you see in him?"

Silence, but it felt like words. Fire clashing between them. She felt her own heartbeat, hard and heavy at the core of her, but could not make herself look away from him. She demanded shakily, "Why are you still here?" Her words were only a whisper and he ignored them.

"You don't strike me as Natham's usual type."

Molly thought of the procession of Saul's blondes and redheads over the years. She would tell him she was Saul's daughter. Tomorrow, in daylight. Not tonight, not with this trembling in her veins.

"You look fresh and young and..." his voice dropped to a suggestive murmur "...too damned innocent for Saul Natham."

She wrapped her arms around herself, found her voice brittle as she said, "Older men have their appeal."

"Do they?" His face seemed harsh and dangerous in the reflected light from below. "But I would think that you——" His voice changed, turned thoughtful. "I don't think I have to worry too much about ethics in this situation."

Her heart lurched. Surely he didn't intend to take her shoulders in his hands again...pull her into his arms and...kiss her...love her. She had not meant to ask, but she whispered, "What do you mean? Ethics?"

He shrugged. "Saul Natham plays around with any woman who has two legs and a set of breasts. He's got to be the least faithful creature on two legs." He moved closer and she lost her breath. "A man needn't feel as if he's stealing anything." He smiled. A shadow smile, disturbing.

"Stealing?"

"Yes, Molly." His voice was a sensual caress on the darkness. "Exactly what you think I mean. You. And me."

Insanity. Wild and impossible, but if he took her in his arms right now she might succumb to the sensual stranger inside herself.

Silence, staring into his shadowed eyes, feeling his touch as if words were physical. When he finally turned away from her, she felt his movement as a pain somewhere deep inside. No words. She watched from above as he went down the staircase to the living room. Dark head, broad shoulders. He stopped and stared back up at her. She could have sworn he could see straight into her thundering heart.

It was dark up here. He could not see. But he did. She knew he did. She heard the door close when he left. Then silence. Was he waiting outside, knowing she would have to come out to her van? When she did, would he enclose her in his arms in the darkness outside? If he opened his arms, would she walk into their trap?

She looked down and saw her hands clenched together. Deliberately, she loosened her grip, slowly felt reason crawling back. Temporary insanity, that was what had happened to her. Molly Natham had never melted, had certainly never *burned* for a man in her life. Until tonight.

No! After twenty-six years of keeping her head, she was *not* going to start making a fool of herself now!

CHAPTER THREE

HE WANDERED through her dreams. There were trees, big cedars with branches drooping down over her, a dark sun, and the shadow of the man.

He was stalking Rex and Bronty, although with their caricature dinosaur fierceness they should have been the hunters.

She ducked behind a tree. Its massive trunk concealed her from the dinosaurs and the black-eyed man. Saul was sitting on a stump, laughing and telling her that the key was in the drawer, but there was a reason for it all. She heard the stranger then, but Saul was gone, no help at all. That was when she realized the stranger was stalking *her*, not Bronty and Rex.

Through the jungle. Pounding, drumming. Drumbeats, warning of the dangers. She heard them, felt them pulsing her blood. He was there, in front of her! She had been running, flying, straight into his arms. He touched her and the sky turned red and hot.

Molly's eyes flew open and she was sitting bolt upright in the bed, the covers tumbled around her, sunlight streaming in. Cold air on her breasts. She shivered and pulled the blankets close. A dream. Of course it had been a dream. Only a dream. Not real, any more than the sense of being pulled into danger last night had been real.

Reality was the pounding. No, the knocking. It must have been magnified by her dream.

Someone at the door downstairs. She stumbled out of the bed, pushed at the sheet that wanted to come with her. So cold. Freezing. She caught up Saul's robe and tied it tightly as she padded down the stairs in bare feet.

She knew who it was before she opened the door. Knocking on the back door seemed so much more intimate than a stranger calling at the front.

"Good morning, Molly."

He was smiling, tall and broad and handsome. He was wearing a pale blue shirt and a darker blue tie, a navy mohair cardigan over dark, immaculate pants. Even his hair was brushed smooth and wavy. Civilized, she thought, and knew she must have imagined last night's wild danger. Her fingers curled around the edge of the door, but she forced herself to stand her ground. She was *not* going to step back and let him in.

"Good morning?" She made it a question and his lips twitched. His eyes dropped to her bare feet, shifting uncomfortably on the cold floor.

"Did I wake you up? Sorry. I brought you some fresh eggs." He held out a carton. "Farm fresh," he added. "And I'm sorry about last night. I guess I must have seemed a bit intimidating."

"Intimidating?" He had haunted her deep with sensual danger. She stared at the egg carton, then her eyes flew up to him, but he was looking at the spot where Saul's robe crossed over her breasts.

His eyes moved to hers, direct and warm. "I'm sorry about last night, Molly. I don't usually hassle my neighbor's guests. And——" He cleared his throat and she had the idea that he actually was embarrassed. "I didn't mean what I said."

She felt herself starting to smile. "You didn't mean your threat to steal me away from Saul?" It was crazy, his thinking she was Saul's latest *affaire de coeur*.

"Did I actually threaten that?"

"It sounded like it." His body language more than the words. That sensation of breathless foreknowledge pulsing through her veins. "Yes, you did, and I'm not anybody's possession, so——"

He stopped her words with a gesture, long fingers spread out to silence her. "I don't—I was having an odd day and . . . well, there was a certain chemistry—still is," he admitted with a low grumble as his eyes strayed again. "Look, this is pretty damned—I am sorry for the melodramatics last night. Will you take the eggs?"

"A peace offering?" Could he hear her heart beating?

"Yes, a peace offering."

"Farm fresh, you said? The eggs, I mean. Do you have chickens?" She grabbed the carton, wishing she could think of comfortable words, conversation. Words seemed like mine fields at the moment. She muttered, "Your clothes don't exactly go with mucking out the chickens."

"My family. The farm down the way." His words were stiff, too. He jerked his head in the general direction of the road.

"The McNaughton farm?"

"That's right. My older brother runs it. I didn't introduce myself last night, did I? I'm Patrick. Patrick McNaughton."

No introduction, but he had held her close against him with one strong arm. She might be dreaming those eyes, the sensation of his arm against her, for years to come.

"No," she agreed. "You didn't introduce yourself."

"All in all, poor hospitality. And Gabriolans have a reputation for hospitality."

"So you came to tell me I'm safe?" Now why had she brought that up again? As if she wanted to walk into danger with him. "Have you—I haven't seen the cat. It didn't come here all night."

"I peeled her off my screen again this morning." His laughter was low and warm. "If you put out some milk, and leave the door open, she may come in. Be careful of her claws, though. She's laid tracks on my arms more than once.''

"I will." She pulled the robe closer around herself. "Thank you. And thank you for the eggs.''

He nodded. "If you have trouble with the water, let me know. Saul was having a problem with the pump.'' He glanced down at her cold feet and frowned. "You have got the heat going, haven't you?''

She shook her head. "There's a wood stove of some sort in the living room, but——''

"Where in Ontario are you from, Molly?''

"Ottawa. And Toronto." His lips twitched and she admitted, "Electric baseboard heaters. I couldn't get the wood to burn.''

"Put something on your feet," he commanded gently. "Socks. Shoes. I'll get the fire going for you.''

She shook her head. "No, I'll—you don't need to.''

"Do you want to shiver all day?''

"No, but——" She frowned. "You'll mess up your clothes.''

"That would be a disaster, wouldn't it?" He laughed. "Go on, get something on your feet." She hesitated and he seemed to read her mind. "Just good neighbors, Molly. Don't worry about it.''

Upstairs, she changed quickly into jeans and a thick sweater, socks and shoes. She could hear little sounds from down below as she hurriedly brushed her hair. When she came down the steps, he was standing up, brushing his hands together. She could hear the crackle of fire, the sound of metal expanding. The stovepipe?

She said hesitantly, "Thank you, Patrick.''

"Close that vent in about ten minutes' time, when it's going well. Then, around noon, open up and add two or three more pieces of wood on top of the coals and it'll keep you warm until this evening.''

"Thank you." She could feel the beginning of warmth radiating, but she made herself walk away from the fire, moving with him toward the back door. "Could I get you to show me some time later? How to start it myself?" She stood, holding the door open for him, not wanting him to leave yet.

"Sure. I'll come this evening." Once outside her door, he turned back to smile at her. "And if you need anything today, my sister Sarah's along the way at the bed and breakfast. You must have seen the sign when you came in yesterday? She could spare you some bread and milk and so forth until you get to the store."

"Thank you." Neighbors. It was a warm feeling.

He said, "I take it back." His voice was strained.

"What? Take what back? The fire?" She shook her head in confusion, knowing that was nonsense.

"I told you I didn't mean what I said last night." He was still brushing his hands absently against each other.

She trembled and whispered, "You mean about taking me away from Saul?"

"This morning I thought I must have been mad, but I was wrong. I meant every word."

"I'm not——" She dragged in a painful breath and found some kind of force behind her words. "I'm not some kind of toy, you know. A possession to—and I'm not interested in——"

"Anyone but Saul?"

"I love Saul." Of course she loved her father, but this was insane, using him as a defense against Patrick McNaughton.

He caught her chin with lean, strong fingers. She could feel his breath on her face. He smelled of soap and fresh, clean male mixed with the faint tang of his after-shave and a breath of wood smoke.

"Why, Molly? Why Saul Natham? He's the most inconstant man alive, and he's far too old for you. You need . . . more than he could ever give you."

She had always needed more than Saul could give, but she was a grown woman now and didn't expect perfection from her father. She should tell him—she should . . .

She knew what was going to happen. Only seconds away. His lips. She could not take her eyes off them until they were too close, then she was staring wide-eyed into his black magnetism.

"I thought your eyes were blue," he murmured in a husky, deep voice. "But they're green, too. They change color like cat's eyes."

She had time enough to step back, but she was motionless, waiting, heart beating, lips parting. His mouth covered hers slowly and she felt herself soften, accepting his caress. Warm, dizzy sensation. His hands were resting on the doorframe, supporting his weight as he leaned toward her. He covered her lips with dry warmth and she trembled deep inside. His kiss was seductive, drawing her deeper. Her heart was thundering, her body drawing closer, needing his arms to take her to him.

When he pulled away from her, she could feel her lungs straining, empty.

"You see?" he demanded huskily, holding her eyes.

"What?" She touched swollen lips with the tip of her tongue.

"Saul isn't the only man who can stir you."

"You're . . . crazy," she whispered. She was aching for him to kiss her again, pull her close. She hugged herself with nervous arms and muttered, "Get out of here. Go away." She felt tension grow like wildness in her veins.

"I'll be back," he said softly. "So expect me, Molly."

She spent the morning trying to shake the feeling that he would return at any moment. Whenever she touched her lips with her fingers, she could feel the soft tingle, the echo of his kiss. A solitary morning, and yet with every sound she jerked and felt her heart thundering.

Patrick McNaughton. Did he actually think she would just open her arms and...? It would be explosive when she did. Shattering. Overwhelming.

When she did?

"Never!" she muttered. She didn't even like him.

That was a lie, but liking had nothing to do with it. Something deep inside her had recognized him, wanted him. It made no sense at all and she would shake it pretty quickly. Chemistry, that was what it was. Some men had it, she supposed, and her new neighbor was certainly one of them.

He had had her at a disadvantage, tired and disorientated from the long cross-country drive, and then this morning—well, she'd just woken up. Hardly fair tactics to kiss her when she was half asleep! It was six o'clock in the morning! He'd woken her up at an unearthly hour. He had a lot of nerve, this neighbor of hers!

She would fry some of his eggs for breakfast. He owed her that much after those dreams last night.

She scrounged around in the cupboards for something to go with the eggs, but found no bread, no crackers, no vegetables. The refrigerator was turned off and it smelled terrible inside. She closed it quickly. There were tins of flour and baking powder on the counter. A gas stove with an oven, but she couldn't figure out how to light the oven, so gave up on the idea of scones for breakfast.

She had the eggs alone, then she found a tin of apple juice in the cupboard over the sink and washed down her breakfast with warm juice.

She found the hot-water tank in the bathroom. It seemed to be gas, too, but the pilot light was out. She had no matches left. How had Patrick lit the fire this morning? She would have to boil water on the stove top to clean, but first she would use that telephone. She still couldn't see where the wires came into the cabin, but Saul had both electricity and telephone up here.

Molly dialled through to Toronto, thinking she would leave money to cover the call, then remembering that it was her house now. She was the lady in residence. She smothered a chuckle knowing that she would eventually find Saul's telephone bills in the mail. She would be the one paying.

Aunt Carla answered on the first ring, demanding, "Molly? Where are you?"

Molly reassured her, but Aunt Carla was still muttering about Saul's inconsiderate ways when the conversation ended, adding a final resentful, "He could have waited for you to get there, at least." Or left a key, added Molly silently, but she wasn't about to add fuel to Aunt Carla's perpetual state of outrage with her brother.

"Don't worry," she reassured Carla. "It's beautiful here. The cabin is gorgeous, electricity and running water and the whole bit, and I'm going to get in a full day's work today, then take a walk through the trees. Anyway, here's the phone number, and hang on to my mail until I figure out the mailing address, would you?"

In Ottawa, her domain had ended at her apartment door. Now Molly wandered in and out of the cabin, locating a bucket, then filling it and scrubbing floors with water heated on the stove top. A full day's work, and Carla would have assumed she meant sketching and painting, not scrubbing Saul's neglected floors.

After she had the kitchen clean, Molly wandered through the cedar stand behind the cabin with a mug of coffee in her hand. Fantastic smells, the tang of cedar mixed with other extravagant, natural scents. Was that a honeysuckle vine tangled in the branches overhead?

Wild mushrooms growing under the trees. She would have to get a book to find out if they were edible.

She heard the telephone ringing and hurried inside to answer it. Aunt Clara calling back, she thought, or one of her father's women friends, wondering where he was and why he had not kept his promises.

"Molly? *Ça va?*"

Molly sank down on to the sofa with the receiver against her ear, smiling at the sound of his voice. "Where are you, Saul?"

"Airport." He was laughing and she shrugged. If he didn't want to say, he wouldn't. He had greeted her in French, which meant he would be *en route* to Montreal or Paris. She knew his ways.

"The cabin's great," she told him. "Thank you."

"Hmm." Saul was always uncomfortable with gratitude. "Has anyone been looking for me? Calling?"

"No. I just got here. Listen, Saul, the cat——"

"Don't tell anyone where I am, will you?" There were sounds around him, anonymous airport sounds.

"How can I? I don't *know* where you are. Who's looking for you? And why?"

"I just need peace and quiet for my painting. Take care, Mo——"

"Saul, hold on! Don't hang up! The mail? How do I get mail? Where? And keys? Where are the keys to the house?"

"Check around, the neighbors will help you out. Next door—— My plane's going. Better fly. And Moll—don't tell anyone where I am."

Was he running from a woman? Usually Saul had the sense to pick women who were as transient as he was, but every now and then he found himself entangled deeper than he wanted to be. She had known there would be some reason for his gift, that it would be more than the impulse to give his daughter a birthday present. Even assuming a woman in hot pursuit, why should Saul give the cabin away? Why not just lock up and go?

The cat? No. Saul wasn't heartless, wouldn't actually abandon the cat forever, but he was quite capable of charming someone into taking over custody without having to give away his home. Molly frowned, knowing that all the hassle of the lawyer and the paperwork of the property transfer was completely out of character for her father.

Why go at all? Why not unplug the telephone and lock the door, ignore any unwanted women who came knocking? She remembered other times, other women coming. Back then it had been Molly who went to the door, sending interruptions away while her father painted and sealed out the world.

If this was another woman problem, Molly would have expected Saul to stay put until his September showing, painting like mad and oblivious to the rest of the world. He said he needed peace and quiet. What did he call this? The rat race?

She went upstairs and worked on clearing away Saul's things, disturbed by the fact that he had left behind his brushes, his oils and his palette. He had told her he needed to paint, but had left behind both his studio easel and his sketching easel. So why——?

She stopped to glance through the tall cathedral windows, searching for the impression of movement she had sensed in the clearing outside.

A deer.

Softly, Molly moved along the narrow walk to the balcony. The animal was motionless on the far side of the clearing, head lifted, ears alert. Molly stopped breathing, wanting to move closer, but afraid movement or sound would panic the golden animal into flight. No antlers. Did that mean it was a female? A doe? It lifted its head and stared directly at Molly, then turned and slowly wandered into the trees.

Saul had promised there would be deer.

A few moments later, Molly found a set of keys in Saul's paint box. Front door key. Back door. A small unmarked key. For a padlock? She shrugged and moved on to the two General Motors keys. Car keys? Where was Saul's car? She shrugged that problem away. It was years since she had trailed behind Saul, keeping track of his keys and his timetable and his finances—all the things he habitually forgot.

With the cabin clean, Molly heated water and took a sponge bath, promising herself that she would figure out the hot-water heater later so that she could shower and shampoo. Then she dressed in clean jeans and blouse, and went to work on the dinosaurs.

She set up the sketching easel on the balcony with the paper tacked to it. Then she attached Alex's latest manuscript to a clipboard so the light breeze could not blow it away. She stared at the manuscript for a moment, then went to the van and brought her portable stereo and cassette case inside. Once she had a tape playing, she went back out on to the balcony with the sounds of Neil Diamond's latest album flowing over her. She always listened to music while she worked.

She hummed tunelessly as she moved about, getting organized, getting into the fantasy mood so that when she picked up the charcoal it was easy to rough out the first picture. She had read the manuscript several times since Alex sent it to her, but she found herself chuckling again as she let the opening scene of *Search for Bronty* take shape on the paper.

Alex had a wild imagination. It was no wonder children loved his stories. A brontosaurus wandering around Mexico City, lost in the *barrios*. His friends, tyrannosaurus Rex and Terry the pterodactyl, searching for him, throwing Mexico City into chaos. The kids were going to love this latest episode in the continuing saga of the modern-day dinosaurs!

Molly had tourist literature spread out around her, pictures of Mexico City tacked on to the rails with clothes pins she had found in Saul's kitchen drawer. As the afternoon went on, she added four rough sketches to the collection of paper around her.

She liked to rough the whole project out before she got down to the detailed artwork. The publisher wanted fourteen illustrations for this book, plus cover art. It was important to choose the right scenes, to distribute the illustrations more or less evenly through the events of the story. The first time Molly illustrated one of Alex's stories, she had painted dozens of illustrations, reorganizing the project as she went, discarding half her work in the end, wasting time and energy. Now, after six dinosaur books, she had developed an efficient work pattern.

Hours later, she was interrupted by a light, young voice. "Hey! Hey, you up there?" The boy was directly below the balcony, his face lifted up, his mouth open and his neck strained back.

Molly lifted her charcoal away from the paper and smiled down at him. "Hello, there."

He was eight or nine years old, his hands jammed into the back pockets of his loose denim jeans. His curly, dark hair and black eyes reminded her strongly of Patrick McNaughton.

His son? She felt an uncomfortable sensation of nausea at the pit of her stomach. Patrick was a stranger, for God's sake! She didn't care if he was married, had children. Although, if he was, he had no business kissing the woman next door. She would tell him so, too, when she saw him next.

"Who are you?" the boy asked, as direct as the man.

"I'm Molly."

"Oh. Where's Saul?"

"Away. Flying somewhere on an airplane."

That seemed to satisfy the boy's curiosity. He nodded wisely and told her, "He's my friend. I came over to see if Trouble wanted petting."

Molly turned the sketching charcoal absently in her fingers. "I haven't seen Trouble all day. She ran away when I came last night. Do you know where she might be?"

The boy threw a glance back toward the trees. "Climbing Uncle Pat's sun room again, maybe. I'll go see if I can get her. Do you have any bacon?"

"Bacon?"

"Yeah, that's what Saul always feeds Trouble."

As a child, Molly had dined on caviar, oysters, sometimes on nothing at all. Hardly ever on hamburger or macaroni. She should have known that Saul would not feed his cat ordinary cat food.

The boy was disappearing into the trees.

"Hey, neighbor! What's your name?"

"Jeremy!" he shouted back, his voice echoing.

Uncle Pat, he had said. Patrick McNaughton was the boy's uncle, although it was stupid of her to be so pleased. He mattered. Too soon, too dangerous, but she was tangled in strange emotions, trying to tell herself she did not care. She had spent most of the day without consciously thinking of his kiss, but it had been there, the tingling excitement of memory lying in wait. He had said he would come tonight, to show her how to light the fire. Would he kiss her again? Would she let him? Or would she draw back from the danger? One kiss, a few seconds engraved on her mind, warm male lips brushing hers. Did he know how her heart had thundered, sending flames through her veins?

He believed she was one of Saul's ladies. Would he think that her response to his kiss meant she would fall into bed with him, that she believed in the kind of easy loving Saul pursued? He might think that, probably did. She would have to tell him who she really was, make it clear that she was not a woman to let a strange man kiss her and...

Except that she *had* let him.

She found a tin of bacon in the back of a kitchen cupboard and started frying a couple of strips. Jeremy had seemed quite certain that Trouble wanted bacon. Voices. Molly swallowed, recognizing the lower tones of Patrick's deep voice contrasting with Jeremy's. She opened the door and there was the cat, locked in Patrick's arms, much as she had been the night before.

"Got her!" announced Jeremy triumphantly.

"Good work," said Molly, avoiding Patrick's eyes but staring at his long fingers curled into the scruff of the cat's neck. "You're hurting her."

Patrick said confidently, "No, I'm not. Don't you know anything about cats?"

"Not much." Saul had never stayed in one place long enough for pets, while Aunt Clara and Uncle Gordon had always lived in a city apartment that didn't allow animals.

"City girl," he taunted gently. "We'll help you settle her in. First we have to be sure all the doors and windows are closed while she gets used to you."

He went past her and Molly closed the door behind him. Patrick said, "Jeremy, check the downstairs windows and so forth. Molly, what about upstairs?"

She shrugged. "The door to the balcony is open."

"Jeremy, get it, would you?"

Molly opened her mouth to protest, but Patrick said quietly, "Don't worry. Jeremy won't touch anything."

The man was a mind reader.

He had changed out of his city clothes into an old pair of denim jeans and a battered University of Waterloo

sweatshirt. If anything, he looked even more disturb-
ingly potent in casual clothes. It was a good thing he
had the cat in his arms, she decided. With that look in
his eyes, he might just reach for her otherwise.

She swung away from him. Somehow, she had to get
this relationship on a better footing. Damn! It wasn't a
relationship. The man's presence seemed to scramble her
brains. When she turned to face him again, she found
that he had made himself comfortable on the living-room
couch, the cat still held in his arms.

"Come over here, Molly."

He seemed so at ease, as if this chemistry between
them were an ordinary thing to him. She thought of Saul,
women tearing their hearts out for him and meaning
nothing in his life. She felt out of her depth, frightened
and vulnerable. She bit her lips and muttered, "Why
don't you sit down and make yourself at home?"

"Come on," he urged, his voice gentle, soft laughter
in his eyes. "You need help with this cat and you know
it. Come and sit beside me."

Molly felt as if she were walking into a mine field!
When she sat down, Trouble glared at her and growled
low in her throat. Patrick's hand shifted on the cat's
neck, his thumb rubbing the side of her jaw until the
angry sound stopped.

Molly laughed uneasily. "I don't think she likes me.
I—am I supposed to touch her?"

"Not yet." Patrick shifted and his leg pressed against
hers. She wanted to move away, but knew it would be
too obvious if she did. Patrick smiled at her and Molly
wondered if he knew how self-conscious she felt.

"Just sit here, Molly. Let her get used to your smell.
Relax."

Did he think she was so tense and awkward because
of the cat? If so, he must think she was pretty stupid.
Or phobic about cats. She swallowed and stared at the

cat, seeing only Patrick's chest in that old sweatshirt. "Did—did you go to the University of Waterloo?"

"Hmm. Just give her jaw a bit of a scratch, rub it a bit."

Trouble tolerated the caress for a few seconds before she jerked her head away. Molly withdrew her hand. The University of Waterloo was in Ontario, perhaps three thousand miles away. "Why go so far when there's UBC right nearby?"

He shrugged and loosened his grip on Trouble. The cat didn't try to get away. "I took my Bachelor's at UVic, in Victoria. Did graduate studies at Waterloo. They were doing interesting things with computers." He saw her grimace and laughed easily. "You don't like computers?"

"That all depends. I like banking machines, but I don't trust them."

He watched her thoughtfully, asked, "Who do you trust, Molly?"

"Not a computer, anyway. I had an argument with one once. Stubborn beasts." Who did she trust? She thought that she might trust Patrick McNaughton, although she did not know if it was instinct or insanity.

He said, "If you put a mistake in a computer system, it doesn't make it right." Then, "Well, Jeremy, is it all clear? Everything closed?"

Jeremy came down off the stairs at a half run. He jerked to a stop in front of the couch and reached to scratch Trouble's ear. The cat tipped its head back and purred. Molly laughed. "She should be your cat. She'll only growl at me."

"Mom won't let me," said Jeremy regretfully. "She says we've got too many animals and—anyway, she's Saul's really." He took a deep breath, shook his dark, curly hair back, then the words tumbled out.

"Molly, on your balcony—there's Rex and Bronty and Terry! It really is, isn't it? I know it's Bronty, for sure.

He's between two big buildings. And—it's them, isn't it? All the dinosaurs from the books?"

"What books?" asked Patrick.

Jeremy said impatiently, "*You* know, Uncle Pat! Remember? *Bronty Goes to Hawaii* 'n *Terry and the Jet Airplane*. You remember, don't you? Molly, they are the same ones, aren't they?"

"Yes."

"Molly Alex!" shouted Jeremy triumphantly. "I *knew* it! You're Molly Alex, aren't you? You wrote all those books! Didn't you?"

"No, I didn't write the stories. Molly Alex is a pen name—a special name just for those books. A man named Alex writes them, and I paint the pictures."

Jeremy sank down on to the floor, cross-legged. "Wow!" he breathed. "Is that a new one upstairs? A new Bronty book?"

"Umm-hmm. It's going to be called *Bronty Goes to Mexico*. The story's already written. I'm just starting the pictures for it."

Patrick shifted and his leg pressed warmly against hers. "Let's feed this troublesome beast something. Cupboard love is the best way to teach a cat where home is. Then you can show me your etchings, Molly."

The last thing she wanted was Patrick McNaughton staring at her sketches. Not that she was self-conscious about letting people see her unfinished work. That sort of temperament was the province of real artists like Saul. But Patrick—he might stare at her pictures and see right into her soul.

Freed, the cat stood and stretched in Patrick's lap, then gave him an outraged glare and slowly walked on to Molly's lap. Molly stroked the black and white fur once, then Trouble jumped across to a nearby easy chair.

"I'll feed her." Molly started to stand up, but it was an old couch. With Patrick's weight on the springs as well as her own, she had sunk far down. Patrick steadied her with a hand and helped her up.

"Thanks," she gasped, moving away from him quickly. Was that laughter in his eyes? Darn the man! Tonight she would be dreaming about his warm, strong hand steadying her hip, his eyes inviting her to tumble back down onto the sofa into his arms.

Dreaming of loving.

She cleared her throat and focused on Jeremy who was staring up at her. "I—I think your uncle would be better off to wait until I'm further along. The dinosaurs look better in color."

Jeremy stumbled to his feet. "They're neat, Uncle Pat. There's no colors, yet, but you can tell just who it is. Terry's flying over the skyscraper in one, and he hits a flagpole. And there's more than the ones pinned up, isn't there, Molly? I didn't want to touch them, but it'd be super to look at them all."

Patrick got up, moving to the wood stove as if he were the person who naturally tended to it, a smile in his voice as he said, "Come on, Molly. We understand about it being unfinished work. Jeremy and I are both true dinosaur lovers."

She stared at his back as he crouched in front of the fire, feeding in wood neatly. When he sank back on his heels and looked up at her, she said with resignation, "I can't imagine what the attraction is for you, but go ahead. Jeremy can show you where they are while I feed the cat. I'll come up and show you the others after I've fed Trouble."

CHAPTER FOUR

WHEN Molly came upstairs to the loft, she found Patrick thoughtfully rubbing his chin with one hand while he stared at the painting on the wall behind the sofa bed. Jeremy was outside on the balcony, his bent head just visible through the window as he studied her dinosaur sketches.

Molly was glad she had made up the sofa bed earlier. The idea of Patrick staring at her tousled sheets was disturbing. That suggestive tension leapt up between them so easily. Hormones, she decided desperately. Perhaps she needed to take vitamins. Or get more exercise. Something. Anything to get back to normal.

"I thought you wanted to look at dinosaurs." She licked her dry lips. "They're out on the balcony."

"What is this?"

"What's what?"

"This painting," he snapped impatiently. A muscle jerked along the side of his neck. "What the hell is it?"

"Niagara Falls."

He swung around to glare at her.

"Saul painted it." Why did Patrick look so angry? She looked at the painting. Beautiful scenery, but lacking Saul's usual emotional impact. Molly remembered the misty falls, the white clouds in the summer sky. She had spent hours staring at the clouds while Saul sketched her. *Head to the right, and stop fidgeting, girl!*

"I *know* it's Niagara Falls!"

"Well, why ask, then?" She glared back at him. "Has anyone ever told you that you're a bad-tempered man?"

Abruptly, the anger was gone. "I'm not, you know. Or I wasn't until I met you. That painting—it's you in the foreground, isn't it?"

"Of course it's me." She grimaced. "I have one of those faces. People I knew as a baby tell me I haven't changed a bit. It's not a compliment, I can tell you."

"You're about ten years old in that picture." He said it as if it were an accusation.

She shifted her shoulders. "I didn't know he still had that picture. I thought he'd sold it."

"How old were you?"

"Twelve."

His fingers curled into a fist. He took a deep breath, then the words came one at a time, with pauses between. "Saul Natham painted this picture when you were twelve years old? Is that right?"

"Yes. He started it on my birthday." The last wandering birthday, before she went to her aunt and uncle.

"On your birthday? Your twelfth birthday?" He closed his eyes briefly, muttered, "Of course he's not your lover. I should have known you were entirely wrong for that. He's never had anyone even remotely intelligent here. And no artists."

She couldn't help smiling at that. "No artists," she agreed. "He doesn't like competition."

"But you——"

"Saul doesn't think of my work as art. Children's pictures."

He prowled to the edge of the loft, stared down at the living room below. "He's your father? Your uncle? What? And why did you tell me he was—that you were his lover?"

Why did she feel so off balance with him? With anyone else, she could be calm and cool. Rational, not emotional. She dragged her fingers through her long, tangled curls. "I didn't tell you that. He's my father. You were the one who assumed I was one of his women."

A muscle jerked in his jaw. "You could have set me straight."

She met his eyes angrily. "I made it a policy a long time ago not to get into a stew over what people think about my father."

"Or about you?"

She nodded abruptly. "Yes. If you judge me before you know anything about me, then that's your problem. I'm not going to let it be mine."

"Damn it, Molly! I spent last night—most of today for that matter—telling myself I had no damned business going after another man's woman."

Her heart was pounding and something inside trembling. Her voice started on a whisper, rose quickly to anger. "Listen, Patrick…Mister bloody McNaughton! I don't know who you think you are, but—you and your family may own the top of this hill, but get this straight! I don't *belong* to anybody!"

He moved toward her. One step. Two. She warned, "Stay away from me! I'm not a possession, for—I told you that last night, damn it! I won't be talked about like some thing, some…I belong to *me*. And I don't— don't want anything to do with you—with your—your— whatever it is you want."

His hands closed over her shoulders. She gasped and tried to jerk away. He said softly, intensely, "Last night you did a damned fine imitation of one of Saul's endless chain of lovers. You knew bloody well what it looked like! What I would think!" His fingers curled into the softness of her upper arms. "And what I want, Molly, is you. It may be crazy. It's certainly too damned soon, I agree." His fingers gentled, thumbs caressing. "We don't even know each other—except I've got the crazy feeling I've known you forever. Anyway, we're going to learn.''

She could have escaped his grasp. His fingers were not hard on her arms, just holding. In a second she would pull away, but now she could only stare up at those incredibly black eyes, her own gaze wide and frightened.

"Don't I have a choice?" Insanity even to ask. She had free will. Certainly she did. He might haunt her here on Gabriola Island, but she could get into her van and drive away. She didn't have to accept Saul's gift, this incredible hideaway on a west-coast island, this man who lived next door.

"Why should you have a choice?" His thumbs caressed the flesh of her arms through her cotton blouse. A warm craving crawled through her veins as he said in a low, compulsive voice, "I had no choice. When I saw you walking across the ferry tarmac, that long-legged walk and those gorgeous black curls—damn it, Molly! I've seen beautiful women before. I don't know why you should have this effect on me, but you do."

His head lowered. She licked her lips, frightened by the thundering of her own pulses. "Jeremy," she whispered. Beautiful, he had said, his voice shaken as if she were somehow more than all the beautiful women. "He'll... You shouldn't..." Her hands pushed against his chest as he brought her closer. She spread her fingers out, pressing against him even as her lips parted. "I didn't..."

His lips cut off her words. Soft heat. He teased until she gave him entry, then he released her arms and traced the curve of her back with his fingers, drawing her closer. She wanted to free her hands to explore the black curls at the back of his neck, the hard muscles that led up from his shoulders. She needed her breasts crushed soft against his hard, broad chest.

He deepened the kiss with seductive slowness, taking the sweetness from her lips, the sultry taste from her mouth. When a wild, low sound escaped her throat, he caught her hands in his and guided them to their rightful place around his shoulders, his neck. She shuddered, feeling his body close against hers, holding her, sheltering and inflaming. Her flesh melted close in a surrender older than time. A promise. A commitment. Not choice, yet not pulled against her will either. Something beyond volition, beyond decision. Inevitable.

She tried to pull him closer when he dragged his lips away from hers. "Molly," he groaned. Her hands were inflaming him with small, convulsive caresses along the back of his neck. "Oh, God, Molly, you——" His eyes closed tightly, then opened. He caught her hands in his and drew them away. "Later," he said raggedly. "Jeremy's going to—another minute of you in my arms and nothing could stop my taking you."

She pulled back. Taking. Wasn't that what her wild blood wanted right now? To be possessed in the oldest way.

"No." Her voice sounded hoarse. "I don't...we can't...don't want..." His eyes reminded her that she had answered his kiss with wildness from somewhere inside. She had pressed her body so close that she was unsure whose heart had been thundering in her ears. His? Or hers? Theirs?

"Did you——" She cleared her throat. "Did you want to see the dinosaurs?"

"Your etchings? Yes, Molly. Please." His voice was quiet, filled with the knowledge of the promise her body had made to him.

She tried to walk across to the balcony as if he were not watching her. She could hear him behind, *feel* him close as if he emanated a radiation she was particularly sensitized too. Perhaps he did. What other explanation could there be?

Out on the balcony, her unwillingness to show Patrick her sketches dissolved as she realized that he was genuinely interested. Jeremy, of course, was a passionate fan of the Molly Alex books, but she hadn't expected Patrick to admire her work. She wasn't sure what she had expected. Perhaps the tolerant scorn Saul had shown when she proudly showed him the painting that had won her an award back at art college?

Patrick was no artist. He obviously had little knowledge of painting or sketching; but he was interested in the process, examining her pinned-up background pictures, the reference books with their detailed plates showing reconstructed creatures of the Mesozoic era.

"No wonder they always look so real," he mused as he turned the pages.

She was amused. "You've read the Molly Alex books?"

"Mmm." He grinned. "Jeremy and his sister have a copy of every known Molly Alex dinosaur book, and my sister Sarah is a great hand at roping dinner guests into reading bedtime stories."

Jeremy declared quickly, "I'm too old for bedtime stories. That was when I was a baby, when Uncle Pat read to me. Now I read for myself." He rammed his hands into his jeans pockets and stared at Molly, willing her to believe in his maturity. "Sally's the baby," he added. "I'll bring her tomorrow, if you like."

Molly offered, "I'll make cookies for you both—or are you too old for cookies?"

"Nobody's too old for cookies!" Jeremy's hands crawled out of his pockets, fingers curling as if he could feel the crumbling cookies in his grasp. "Can we come right after school?"

Patrick frowned. "Isn't tomorrow the day Sally's going to Ellie's birthday party?"

"Oh, yeah."

Jeremy's lips turned down until Molly invited, "Just you, then, Jeremy. And I'll bake extra for you to take home to Sally."

Patrick glanced at his watch. "Suppertime for you right now, scamp."

Jeremy turned to go and Molly's hands made a vague motion of protest. Jeremy would go, leaving her alone with Patrick. And then...

"Thanks for helping with the cat!" she called after the boy.

Patrick added, "And don't let her out when you go!"

Molly asked, "Aren't you going with him?"

"Do you want me to go?"

Molly swallowed and avoided Patrick's eyes. She moved restlessly, her hands collecting the pictures tacked up on the balcony rail and her mind in chaos.

"Can I help you clear up?"

She nodded. The pictures. The paints. The easel. She shook her head, but he held out his arms and she placed the small pile of papers in them. Then she picked up the easel and he followed her into the loft. Inside. Alone.

The telephone was ringing as they came in. She set the easel down and ran downstairs, picking the receiver up and saying "Hello?" breathlessly.

"Molly, I want you do something for me."

"Saul——" She could hear Patrick moving around upstairs. Bringing in the rest of her things? "What is it? Where are you?"

"Get my canvases together, would you? Be careful, for heaven's sake! I don't want any damage——"

"What canvases?" Molly twisted as her eyes scanned the downstairs walls. "The only painting I've seen is the one over the sofa upstairs. You know? Niagara Falls. The one——''

''No, no! Not that one. There's a cupboard in the eaves. I had a builder in to make some racks. You'll find them. Seventeen canvases. Babette will be there tomorrow to pick them up.''

''Babette?'' Trust Saul, she thought with a wild giggle. ''Where are you?''

''Molly, I haven't got time for this nonsense. Just pack them up, girl, and stop putting me through the inquisition. Ten o'clock.''

''In the morning? Seventeen paintings? And pack them in what? Have you got anything to wrap them with here? If not, I'll have to go into Nanaimo.''

Saul gave an explosive sigh. ''Stop making difficulties. If I know Babette, she'll be late anyway. Enjoy yourself, Molly. I'll be in touch.''

Molly replaced the receiver slowly. ''Enjoy myself,'' she muttered. ''Seventeen paintings hiding in the eaves, and I'm to get them ready instantly.''

''Everything okay?''

She jerked at the sound of Patrick's voice. He had warm amusement in his eyes, as if he knew that she had forgotten he was here, knew how her pulse had leapt at his voice.

''That was your father, wasn't it?'' She nodded, but he was frowning. ''Does he always dump tasks on you at the last minute?''

She shrugged, saw the look in his eyes and stepped back.

''Are you afraid of me, Molly?''

She didn't answer.

''Come here, then,'' he commanded gently.

She shook her head.

He considered her silently for a moment. ''Come outside for a walk, then. I'll show you my place.''

"Patrick, I——" What did he expect of her? Passion? Making love? After that kiss upstairs, did he believe that she would tumble into a bed with him? "I——" She shivered, knowing that it was not saying no that bothered her. It was wanting to say yes, yet not even knowing *how*. She turned and moved restlessly away from him, then swung back suddenly. If he touched her, her mind would turn to jelly again. "I'm not——"

He waited, one hand slid into his pocket, the fingers of the other curled, not exactly tense. Just waiting.

The lump in her throat was growing. "I—Patrick, I think you've—well, you—maybe I——"

"Just say it, Molly."

His chest was rising and falling in a slow, steady movement. Steady, like the man. Solid. Passionate underneath. There had never been anyone like this in her life. She could not understand what it was that made him believe he wanted her, could not let herself trust it. "I—if you think—well, what happened up there... upstairs... I——"

"Just spit it out."

"Well——" She made a rough, uncertain motion with her hands. "I'm... not in the habit of having casual affairs."

"Casual, Molly?"

Her heart crashed against her ribs. "You know what I mean." She bit her lip and added weakly, "Don't you?"

"You want me to slow down?" He brushed her cheek with the side of his thumb, then tucked a wild black curl behind her ear. "You feel it, don't you, Molly? This pull between us?"

"Yes," she whispered. Was she insane, believing this man to be her fate? Wanting it to be true.

A muscle worked at his temple. "Do I have time to go slow, Molly? How long are you staying on Gabriola?"

Forever. Her lips parted to say the word, but Molly knew better than to believe in forever. She gulped and asked, "What do you want from me?"

"I'm not sure." His fingers threaded through her hair. "How long are you staying, Molly? Long enough for us to find out what this is between us?"

A shudder crawled along the nerves of her scalp. Her fingers spread on his chest. "Saul gave me this house," she said unsteadily. "A . . . birthday present. That's why I came. To . . . to live in it."

He let out a slow breath and Molly moved away abruptly.

"Molly——"

"I—where does the power come from? It's not magic, is it? The electricity, I mean. Getting to this house with no wires."

He dropped his hand and she realized that he had decided not to come after her, not to touch and send her pulses racing. Not yet, anyway. He said, "Not magic. The man who built this place laid all the services into an underground conduit. Will you have dinner with me tomorrow. At my place?"

"You're not . . . married or anything?"

"No. What about you?" She shook her head and he said, "There's no one to object then, is there? Dinner tomorrow?"

"I—could we—somewhere public?"

He was amused. "You don't trust me to keep my hands off?"

She flushed. "You've been living next door to Saul, watching his love life parade past. I know what he's like. I—but just because I'm his daughter I—it doesn't mean I'm willing to go to bed with you." She looked away from the disturbing flash of emotion in his eyes. "I just want you to understand that if—well, if that's what you want, you—you're wasting your time."

* * *

She kept hearing that lie. Her voice, her words, over and over again through the evening that followed. Patrick should have laughed. Instead he had made a strange comment about it being her eyes that haunted him, not just her body, then he had left her without repeating that kiss.

She was twenty-six years old, but she had never been tempted by a man before. It wasn't that she hadn't dated plenty of them. Dinner and dancing, friends like Alex who was fun to work with, like Thomas who was quiet and steady and comfortable. There had been male friends and casual dates in and out of her life from the time she was sixteen. Kisses, too, for heaven's sake! Friendly kisses, warm, sometimes even the soft foreshadowing of desire.

She had not known that her blood could boil, had always assumed the passion and the wildness all belonged to Saul, that she had inherited none of it. When she had thought of making love with a man, it had been a shadowy future. A gentle possession. Maybe someday, if she found someone she felt safe with.

Although she loved her family and her friends, she had never had an intimate relationship with a man. A love affair was too much like an echo of Saul's chaotic life. As for marriage, she had turned down three proposals without a second thought. With Saul for her role model, what chance had she to make a marriage work? Her own mother was back before memory. Granted, there were Aunt Carla and Uncle Gordon, the parent substitutes of Molly's teenage years, but why take chances when she was happy enough living alone? All her life she had played it safe, keeping her world as stable as she could amid the chaos Saul had created around her.

The end of an era, she thought wryly, staring at a nude she'd just pulled out of the racks of paintings.

Safety blown all to hell. The sensible thing would be to wrap up these pictures, give them to Babette tomorrow, then pack up her van and start driving east. Saul could keep his cabin. The price of this gift was too high for Molly to pay.

That would be the sensible plan, and Molly was a sensible girl. But...

The next morning, she flipped idly through the telephone book as she waited for Babette. She found Gabriola's small section, located three listings under the name McNaughton. Patrick's second initial was D. David? Daniel? Douglas? She would ask him. She scanned the rest of the page. Medical clinic. Her heart skipped a beat. She was going to stay. And Patrick...

If she was going to lose her head, she would do it sensibly, take precautions first. After Babette had come, she would call for a doctor's appointment. Meanwhile, she would get some work done.

Babette came at eleven, an hour late. Molly heard the car wheels crunching on the drive and walked along the catwalk to the balcony, her charcoal in one hand, the other pushing her hair back from her face. She had searched the boxes in the van, but hadn't yet found the combs she used to hold her hair back when she was working. Meanwhile, her hair was curling all over her face, messy and troublesome.

The blonde slammed the door of the large station wagon and Molly found herself staring straight down at the woman's deep, exposed cleavage.

"Babette? I'll be down in a second."

"Hi, honey! Take your time." Babette had a slight drawl that made her pleasant voice seem deeply suggestive. Trust Saul, thought Molly with amusement.

Once inside, Babette looked around critically. "Not very big, is it? Have you got a Scotch?" She held out the car keys to Molly. "I could use a long one while you load up those paintings."

Molly eyed the high heels and decided that Babette wasn't the type to carry things without dropping them. Saul would never forgive her if any of his paintings were damaged. For that matter, Babette would probably break an ankle on the stairs to the loft, if she were persuaded to help. So Molly would load the paintings herself.

She said neutrally, "No Scotch, I'm afraid. There is some wine, though."

The older woman sat on the couch with a bottle and a glass, while Molly carried four bundles of paintings down the stairs and out to the station wagon. She had wrapped each painting with a layer of plastic bubbles, then tied the canvases together in bundles of four or five, the plastic protecting the delicate cargo from damage from the string or the neighboring canvases. Saul must have bought a truckload of the bubbles. One end of the eaves had been full of the stuff, the other end occupied by canvases neatly stored in racks.

"Exciting, isn't it?" drawled Babette, following Molly outside with the last bundle. "Just like being in a movie."

Molly carefully placed the bundle of canvases. "Is it?" she asked idly as she closed the tailgate. Babette had been talking from the moment she came, meaningless chatter every time Molly walked past. Molly had stopped listening. The woman had a brain the size of a pea.

Babette took the last drop of wine directly from the bottle, then handed the empty bottle and the glass to Molly, accepting her keys in return. "I never thought I'd get to be a *fugitive*."

Molly choked. "*You're* a fugitive?"

"Not me, silly." Babette's laughter rang out low and husky. The woman might not have any brains, but she certainly had a nice voice. "Sauley's the fugitive. Why do you think I'm smuggling these paintings to him?"

Molly stared after the station wagon as it backed down the uneven driveway. Sauley? Saul? Her father a fugitive? Smuggling the paintings?

"I don't believe it," she whispered. "I don't. She's nuts."

Something soft rubbed against Molly's ankles. She looked down and found the missing cat twisting between her legs. "Hi, there," she whispered, bending down to scratch Trouble's ear. The cat jerked back and hissed at her. She laughed and said, "Make up your mind, kitty." Surprisingly, when Molly turned and went back into the house, the cat followed at a distance.

Her father wasn't a criminal. He was artistic and compulsive. Passionate. Some people would say he was crazy. But not criminal.

A fugitive.

It must be a joke. And the smuggling thing, that was just a loose way of speaking. Babette's conversation was mostly senseless babble. Paintings took up a lot of room. You couldn't smuggle seventeen canvases all that easily. Especially, a dimwit like Babette couldn't smuggle them.

You could take a canvas off the frame and roll it, thought Molly uneasily. No! The whole thing was stupid. Babette hadn't made a bit of sense until that last bit, but it wasn't the way it sounded.

Molly shrugged it away and went back upstairs. She had just started sketching the detailed outline for the first illustration when the telephone rang.

"Molly, it's Patrick."

She had known the instant she heard his voice. She sank down, smiling. "Are you at work? I hear bustle."

"Hmm. A wild day. I'm tempted to pack up and work at home today." Her heart skipped a beat, but his voice went on hurriedly, "Look, I didn't give you any idea of what to wear, did I? I thought we'd have dinner at the

White Hart. It's a neighborhood pub on the island. Informal. Friendly. A good kitchen.''

"I know." She coiled the telephone wire around her finger. "I had dinner there the day I came to the island. I'll wear a skirt and blouse, something casual."

"Whatever you like," he agreed. "Jeans, if you want. Anything short of a formal dress would be in place. I'll pick you up at seven."

It was thoughtful of him to realize that she might be uncertain what would be appropriate dress. She added that to the little things she was learning about Patrick McNaughton. Day three, she thought, and she knew that he had a younger sister whose children he read bedtime stories to. An older brother who worked a neighboring farm. He wasn't married, although he was certainly eligible. Had he ever been married? How old was he? Mid-thirties, she decided. And successful. Something to do with computers, although he wasn't like some computer people she had met, fanatical and unable to talk about anything else.

He had the house next door to hers, but she had never seen it. He was handsome, muscular, tall enough that Molly had to look up. She rather liked that. Strong, but he used his strength carefully. Considerate.

He wanted her, seemed quite determined to pursue her. Molly hadn't done much to discourage him. Didn't want to discourage him, although she knew that once he got to know her he would find her pretty ordinary. Did he think Saul Natham's daughter would be exciting? In the end, he would realize that whatever had attracted him so strongly was just an illusion. What had he said he liked? Her hair. Her eyes. Her walk. He liked her dinosaur pictures, but that surely wasn't the foundation of a serious relationship.

"Lighten up, Molly," she muttered as she drew an angry line on the sketch. Poor Bronty was supposed to be looking excited in this picture, but Molly had turned him into a wistful and unhappy creature.

She would wear the cranberry-colored skirt with its dozens of tiny pleats. And the black silk blouse with a scarf tucked into the neck to match the skirt. Would Patrick like her in that outfit? She could pin the scarf with the gold leaf-shaped pin Saul had given her for her eighteenth birthday. She had bought earrings to match it last year in Toronto.

She dropped her charcoal and stared at the picture of Bronty. She would have to start again. She'd better start getting somewhere with these illustrations. She'd lost almost a week packing up and driving out here. She couldn't afford to lose another week thinking about the man who lived next door. This was her livelihood and she had a deadline.

Bronty started to take shape again on the easel, the new outline sketched in over the old. Both would be covered when she started painting over with her acrylic colors. The prehistoric beast stared out at her inquisitively from the rough lines of the skyscrapers.

At her ankles, Trouble moved back and forth, rubbing and making hungry noises. Molly would have to ask Patrick if there was somewhere on the island to buy cat food. The bacon was gone now. Trouble had turned her nose up at Molly's offering of a dish of milk. Weren't cats supposed to like milk? Would Trouble eat cat food if it was offered? Or did it have to be bacon? She must ask Jeremy this afternoon.

Jeremy! He was coming over after school, and Molly had promised cookies. That meant she had to figure out that oven, and quickly.

Was there a chance that Patrick McNaughton might actually fall in love with her? And perhaps stay in love?

CHAPTER FIVE

THE White Hart was pulsing pleasantly with the beat of a guitar as Patrick held the door open for Molly. The waitress smiled and greeted him by name, then glanced curiously at Molly.

Patrick said, "We've come for dinner. I promised Molly the best food on the island."

The waitress laughed and led them to a small table in a corner. Patrick ordered a Perrier and Molly asked for one too. "Have something stronger if you want," he offered when the waitress was gone. He smiled and admitted, "I thought I'd better keep my inhibitions about me. You said you wanted to take it slowly."

It had been easy enough to theorize about losing her head with this man when she was safely alone. Now, with his eyes on her and her mind painting erotic pictures at the sound of his voice, she was terrified. His voice was so casual, talking about taking it slowly, making it obvious that he could turn his reactions on and off at will. She knew that she was going to make a complete fool of herself over him, could not seem to stop herself. Why couldn't she stay the way she had always been before? Cool and calm. Careful.

She stared at the table in front of her and muttered in a low voice, "I don't want an affair."

He covered her hand with his, somehow brought her eyes up to meet his. "Molly, the affair's inevitable. You know it as well as I do. We can take it slowly." His voice was low, pitched for her ears only. She felt a shiver travel along her arm from the place where his fingers covered hers. "That is, we can try to slow it down. As for denying it—you're crazy if you think that's possible."

She stared at their linked hands and whispered, "I don't want to talk about this." She swallowed and added tightly, "This is—I—I don't even know you."

The waitress delivered their drinks and their menus. Molly freed her hand from Patrick's. On the other side of the room, the guitar player burst into a moody song. Molly hummed along quietly and tried to concentrate on the menu. Oysters? Or tacos? A burger that she knew was positively gourmet? Patrick, watching her as if she fascinated him.

"Tell me about yourself, Molly. How did you become the dinosaur lady?"

"Accidentally, really." She shrugged and let the menu drop to the table. "Until I was twelve, I lived around painting all my life. The idea of doing anything else seemed impossible." She grinned. "I had the idea that I'd be another famous artist like Saul. Only, by the time I'd been a couple of years at the college of art, I knew I didn't have it in me. I'm competent, but whatever it is that Saul's got—— Well, maybe I don't want it," she admitted ruefully. "It drives him, and I like my life under control. You don't want to hear all this."

"You're wrong. What happened when you were twelve?"

She picked up her glass and turned it in her fingers. The sides of it were cool. The man with the guitar was telling a tale of love gone wrong and a hard-hearted woman. The group of four at the next table were arguing heatedly about a rumor that there might be a bridge built to connect Gabriola to Vancouver Island.

Molly asked, "Why would you want to know?" just as a man at the next table said loudly,

"Real islands don't have bridges!"

"Because I find everything about you fascinating."

"Oh." She licked her lips. His eyes were asking hers to lift, but she would not let it happen. "I went to live with my aunt and uncle. Aunt Carla thought I needed stability."

"Did you want to live with them?"

"Yes, but I missed my father." She shrugged that off and added hurriedly, "Saul's not that good at remembering what's not in front of him at the moment." She shook her head, knowing her thoughtless comment was more revealing than she had intended.

He said quietly, "You were lonely."

"Busy," she corrected. He had found his way through too many layers of her secret self already. She smiled and said lightly, "Aunt Carla believes in keeping children busy. She doesn't have any of her own, but her theories are quite definite. She's quite a lady."

Patrick nodded, letting her evasion pass without comment. "So tell me about the dinosaurs."

"I don't usually talk about it."

"I know. You don't usually talk about yourself at all. You'll have to learn, for me."

How did he know that? She turned the glass and he took it out of her hand. Her fingers curled in on themselves and he took her hand to trap her restlessness. "The dinosaurs," he insisted.

Her lips twitched. "Stubborn, aren't you?"

"Mmm." He was smiling, though.

She answered his smile. "All right. I met Alex while I was at art school. He was dating my roommate, taking a creative writing degree at the university. He'd already written two children's books, was determined he could sell them with the right illustrator to work with him." She smiled ruefully. "His fantasy world appealed to me. Maybe a latent childhood interest in dinosaurs. We made a deal and I did the pictures on spec. The whole thing worked amazingly well. The week before I graduated, Alex and I got our first advance check.''

The waitress appeared and Molly picked up the menu again. "Oysters," she decided, then wondered if Patrick had meant to order the oysters all along, or if he echoed her choice because...

That was silly, but it seemed one more thread drawing her to Patrick McNaughton.

He asked quietly, "Are you and Alex lovers?"

She shook her head. "No. Just friends. We were never——''

"Are you in love with him?" His voice was quietly harsh.

Behind Molly, a woman's voice declared with grim authority, "Take us out of the Islands Trust and what'll happen? Gabriola will turn into one big condominium! Move the ferry terminal here and we'll be nothing more than a bedroom for Vancouver!"

Molly said quietly, "Alex married Brenda, my art school roommate. Most of our work, we do together at a distance, by mail." He was waiting for the answer to his question and she found herself confessing, "No. I've never been in love with anyone, not that kind of loving. Just friends. And family." The other voices faded away to leave a world that was only Patrick's eyes, black and magnetic on hers. Words. Silent words.

"Have you?" she whispered.

"You," he said slowly. "I think I'm falling in love with you."

The spell was sharply interrupted by a voice calling across the room. Patrick leaned back, holding Molly's eyes for a second before he turned to face the lean, tall man hurrying toward their table.

"Hey, Pat! I've been trying to get hold of you all week. Where the devil have you been?"

If Patrick minded the interruption, it didn't show on his face, or in his voice as he introduced Molly to Gary Frolward.

"Hi, Molly." Gary's cheeks puffed out as his lips widened. "Sorry to burst in, but I've been chasing Patrick here all week. Pat, I want to talk to you about that candidacy."

"Another time, Gary. Molly and I are having dinner. Politics aren't on the menu."

Gary dropped into the empty chair between them, a thin, intense man in a business suit. "Pat, this is important. That by-election is being called next week. Drummer's going to step down. That's certain. Molly, you don't mind, do you?"

Molly shook her head.

Patrick murmured, "You're asking for it."

"That's a girl, Molly. He's been avoiding me for days." Gary grinned at her as he got back to his feet. "Just keep him in the mood while I go fetch my drink. I'll be right back."

Patrick shook his head ruefully. "Next time," he promised Molly, "I'll take you somewhere else."

"Somewhere you won't be recognized?"

"Somewhere I can hold you in my arms and dance with you. Here he comes. You're about to learn more than you ever wanted to know about British Columbia politics."

"Who is he?"

"Hard to describe. Gary's a creature of politics. Campaign manager sometimes. Lobbyist. Media expert, that being his regular job."

Gary was shortly joined by three others, two men who turned out to be a lawyer and an accountant. A few moments later a blue-jeaned woman named Edie joined the group. Molly was startled to learn that Edie was a bank manager.

"Not my banker's clothes," she admitted with a laugh when she saw Molly's surprise. "I'm human off duty."

"And behind her desk," put in the accountant.

Molly was fascinated by the conversation that flew around the table. Patrick's friends, she had thought at first, and they were. But they were more than friends. They were people concerned about recent environmental issues, involved in trying to exert political pressure to ensure that industry be forced to comply with pollution legislation.

Listening to Patrick's comments, it was no surprise to learn that the others were trying to persuade him to run for political office in a forthcoming by-election.

"You're a natural," said the accountant who was something in the local party executive. "You know everyone in the area—or at least, they all know who you are. Your family's lived here forever. No skeletons in your closet."

"None you know of, anyway," countered Patrick with a laugh.

"Right, and you've got the business sense. You're a good speaker. Not just in front of a crowd, which is bloody important. I heard you addressing the graduating class at NDSS last year, so you can't deny that. You had everyone in that audience in the palm of your hand. But you also come across well with the media. I saw that interview last month on CTV."

Patrick shook his head. "That's all words, John. Nice compliments, but I want you to feel out Sam Nellish first. I think he'd be a better man."

"He doesn't want it," said Edie. "And he looks like a fool on television."

Patrick sighed. "I'm not sure I want it either. I'm not getting pushed into this without thinking it over." Gary's lips parted on a protest and Patrick said firmly, "No more tonight. I'll tell you my decision in a week." He grinned then, catching Molly's hand with his, caressing the backs of her fingers with his thumb. "Enough for one night, friends. Take your pressure group elsewhere. I want to spend some time alone with my lady!"

His lady, as if she had a special place in his life. Laughing, the lawyer and the accountant and the bank manager went away. Gary opened his lips for a parting shot, but Patrick shook his head and even the media expert left them alone.

"They're quite a bunch," she said finally.

"Hmm. A bunch of manipulators, that is." He sounded tolerant, as if they were people he respected. He turned Molly's hand in his. "Shall we leave?"

"Are you a manipulator, too?" She supposed he must be. From listening tonight, it seemed Patrick had founded the largest computer consulting firm on Vancouver Island, that he was currently expanding in all directions and had just bought into a major North American database service.

"Sometimes," he admitted. "I'll admit that I'm trying to manipulate you into my arms, but if you'll come away with me now I'll take you for a moonlit walk and I promise I won't take anything from you that you're not willing to give."

What could she say? That she was torn between willingness and nervousness? That when he looked at her like that she felt so willing that it left her frightened of her own needs?

They drove back along the island in silence. Molly watched Patrick, seeing the hard line of his jaw, the silhouette of his dark moustache. She liked the moustache, liked the look of it, the feel of it stirring the nerve endings of her upper lip. What would it feel like on her body, his kiss, those short, full hairs caressing her heated skin?

She liked the man inside, too. Liked him more with each detail she learned about him.

He turned the car to drive up the hill. Turned again, and again. His Corvette crawled up a long tree-lined driveway and finally came to rest. There was moonlight on the clearing in front of the house. A cedar house, she thought. Warm brown. A rambling affair, a modern version of an older farmhouse style. It would be Patrick's house, and it belonged here among the trees, on the top of a hill that looked out over mountains in the distance. She turned to stare at the lights on some distant mountaintop.

"That's Grouse Mountain on the mainland," he said quietly. "The lights are the chair lift and gondola up to the ski slopes."

"Is this your house?"

"Yes." He opened the car door. She sat frozen in the seat until he came around and opened her door. He reached in his hand and she found herself taking it, letting him help her out. "This isn't a trap," he said seriously. "I said a walk, and there's a path at the back of the house. It's a pretty walk in the moonlight. If we're lucky, we might see some deer."

"Oh."

He closed her door and took her hand firmly in his. "You thought I was going to maneuver you into the house. Seduce you."

"I—yes." He must think her a fool. A hesitant twenty-six-year-old virgin. There couldn't be many of those around these days.

"It crossed my mind," he admitted. "The idea's tempting, to take you in my arms and see if we don't end up in my bed." He drew her hand through his arm. "For tonight, you're safe," he promised. "Don't count on tomorrow, though. When I proposed this walk, I didn't stop to think about your footwear. Shall we go by your place first so you can change?"

"Is it rough going?" She wished she had the nerve to tell him she wasn't sure she wanted to be safe.

"Not really. It's been dry lately, so there won't be any mud. No bushwhacking. We'll stay on the path. Are you warm enough, though?"

"I think so." She had a light jacket that matched the skirt, but the night air was cool enough that she had already drawn the open front of the jacket together for warmth. "Maybe I should get my other jacket from the cabin."

"Hold on a second." He disappeared into his house, taking the steps up to the big veranda two at a time, returning a moment later with a bulky down-filled jacket. "Try this. Here, I'll put your jacket in the car."

His jacket felt warm and secure. "I must look like a balloon," she decided, laughing when he turned to look at her. "Don't you ever lock your car? Or your house?"

"Not often. And you look gorgeous, although the jacket rather drowns you. Come on, before I change my mind and carry you off into my lair."

"I'm too heavy."

He laughed, drawing her arm through his. "Want to bet? Have you ever seen a deer by moonlight?"

"No. The only deer I ever saw was yesterday, from my balcony. Except on television, that is."

"I'll try to find you one tonight."

The path led off toward the right from the back of Patrick's house. Molly glanced at the torn screen that showed in the light from the veranda. Patrick said, "That's Trouble's doing. Saul named her well."

"I'm sorry. I'll pay for it, if you want."

"Don't be ridiculous! I don't want money from you." He shrugged off his irritation with a laugh. "How is the beast? I haven't seen her climbing my screen windows, so I assume you're winning her over."

Molly grimaced. "Sort of. She's accepting food, but complaining about the menu. She let me pet her once this afternoon, and she ate three of the cookies I made for Jeremy. Do cats eat cookies?"

"Apparently this one does. Careful, here, the ground drops." He guided her down, then took her hand loosely in his, swinging their arms gently as they walked on.

Molly breathed in the springtime scent of evergreens and honeysuckle. "Tell me about the farm. You grew up on it, didn't you?"

"Mmm." His fingers linked through hers as he offered, "I'll show you if you like. Tomorrow's Saturday. Why don't you come around with me to meet the family? I'll get David to show you the farm. It's his domain."

If she was going to get embroiled in a flaming affair, why didn't she have the sense to keep a little distance? Share his bed, perhaps, but no more. The more she let herself become entangled in his life, the harder it would be when it ended.

"David's your older brother?" she asked, knowing it was already too late. "Tell me about your family, your childhood."

"Not exciting," he said, but she asked questions as they walked, and Patrick told her about his childhood on the farm, about his fights with his older brother, who he obviously admired. "There was only room for one boss on the farm," he said wryly. "But neither David nor I was willing to shut up and go the other's way. Luckily, I was more interested in computers than cows. So I took business instead of agriculture at university, and we've managed to stay friends as well as brothers."

"He lives at the farm?"

"Yes, and my parents, although nowadays they spend a lot of time away. They have a motor home and they winter down in Arizona. They won't be back until the beginning of June. Often there's just David and Stanley on the farm. Stanley's David's son, eighteen and living for his guitar. He's a good kid—away at university right now.''

''David's wife——''

''Died three years ago. Cancer.'' She squeezed his hand, because there were no words for grief. Patrick said, ''They had the kind of love that warmed everybody around them. It tore Dave up when Sandy got sick. Stanley, too.'' He sighed. ''It was hard on all of us, but— my brother's a hell of a guy. After the funeral, he told me he was lucky. He said fifteen years of happiness was a lot more than most people get, and he'd had the woman he loved for fifteen years.''

They walked in silence, and slowly Molly started to hear small sounds from the trees. '''Coons,'' said Patrick.

''Not bears?''

''No, don't worry about bears. Or cougars, for that matter. There aren't any on Gabriola. Just deer and raccoon and birds.''

And moonlight. It was a magical forest. They had left the path to turn on to a narrow, unused road that Patrick told her had once been a logging road. They followed it through the trees until Patrick suddenly stopped and drew her against him with an arm around her shoulders.

She looked where he pointed and found herself watching a silhouette in the clearing. It moved, turning, and a flash of white tail showed at its rump. A deer. Molly breathed shallowly through her mouth, trying to be silent, motionless, not to frighten the animal. She saw motion to its right and realized that there were two of them, grazing in the small meadow just ahead of her and Patrick. Patrick moved and took her with him, two steps further, and she could see now that there were three of them. A family.

For long, quiet moments, Molly and Patrick watched. Then the largest of the deer moved away toward the trees and the other two followed.

"They're beautiful," she whispered.

Patrick took her chin in his hand and covered her lips with his.

Sweet, the taste of the outdoors mixed with his own heady, masculine scent. She leaned against him, her lips soft under his, her tongue stirring to his touch.

Her fingers moved restlessly at the back of Patrick's neck and his arms tightened in response, drawing her close until she could feel her breasts crushed against his chest, even through the bulky jacket. He deepened the kiss and her breathing turned ragged. His hands, so firm, exploring the shape of her hips below the jacket, then pulling her close.

He slid his hands along her hips, made her mouth tremble under his lips and moved to taste her cheek and the curve of her jaw. "I've got to be crazy, trying to fight this!" he growled softly against the tender flesh of her throat. "I want you," he told her raggedly. "I need you, Molly. Now."

She trembled closer, unable to suppress a soft groan as his need pressed against her. "My lady," he had said to Gary earlier, as if he had known he could claim her. Her arms tightened around his neck as he slid the jacket's zipper down. She gasped softly as his lips caressed through the silk. Pulses going wild in her throat for him, then flames bursting high as his hands slid over the silky curves, seducing her woman's fullness with his touch.

His breath went short as a formless sound escaped her lips and the hard button of her arousal peaked against his palm.

"Molly..."

The softness flared to urgency. He found the scarf at her neck and became lost in its complicated knot. He closed his eyes tightly, drowning in her scent, her feel, groaning, "I can't take you out here in the cold."

"Patrick...I..." He made her lose track of her words with his hands on the beautiful contours of her breast.

"Molly," he whispered. "I want you here, under the stars, naked in the moonlight. I want to see you." He buried his face in the silk-clad softness of her breasts. "I need to know what will happen to your eyes when I kiss you here, whether you'll make that breathless sound...whether..."

She shivered and breathed his name. "Not here," he said painfully. "Not here." He drew in a harsh breath and abruptly let her go. "Molly——" He tried to get his breathing, his heartbeat, under control, concentrated on doing up the zip of the jacket she wore. What was she thinking? A moment ago she had whispered his name in that shaken, passion-loaded voice, but now she was so quiet, so still.

"Molly, will you stay with me tonight?"

She shivered. He had touched her until she was trembling and aching, whispering his name, almost begging him to love her. Then he had stepped back, when she wanted only to drown in his arms. The harshness in his moonlit face frightened her now. It would end with pain. She knew that, but she whispered, "Yes. I'll stay with you tonight."

The air went out of his lungs. He held out his hand. "Let's go back, then," he suggested softly. "I'll show you my place."

She wished it could be more than this, that she could be enough for him forever. But she must not shadow the loving with the pain to come. She put her hand in his and suggested softly, "Come into my parlor?"

"Mmm." He was smiling. She couldn't see his face now that they were turned away from the moon, but the smile was in his voice. "Do you feel like a fly, Molly?

You don't look like one.'' He stopped and kissed her on the lips, a hot, hard kiss that told her more than words could.

She felt alive, her nerves zinging with sensation, her heart racing with joy. For the first time in her life, she did not give a damn about tomorrow. *I want you.* She hadn't the courage to say the words.

She said, ''I feel like a woman.''

''Oh, God, Molly!'' His hands tightened on hers. ''Do you know what you do to me?''

Her lips parted and he covered them again with his, murmuring, ''Are you a sorceress, lady?''

Maybe. Just for one night. For him.

The walk back was magical, moonlit. Patrick told her about his house. He had built it himself over a period of four years, had enjoyed doing it and felt no desire to live anywhere else.

''Mind you, I enjoy traveling.'' He smiled down at her and she saw the white of his teeth in the moonlight, his dark eyes a mystery the moon would not penetrate. ''Coming home is always good for me. There's nowhere quite like Gabriola.''

She understood, looking in from outside. ''It's your home, part of your identity. Roots. It must be a good feeling.''

He squeezed her hand. ''Your home now, too. Saul gave you the cabin.''

''He did, but——'' Knowing Saul, he could easily come asking for it back. And it would be foolish to believe that she could become the woman Patrick McNaughton came home to.

''But what? A gift is a gift.''

Patrick might have been her father's neighbor, but she doubted if he realized how erratic Saul could be. After years of shrugging off the people who criticized her for her father's wild nature, she painfully needed Patrick to think well of her.

"Roots take time," she said lightly. "Maybe you have to be born with them."

"And you weren't?" His voice told her that he was frowning now.

"My father and roots are mutually exclusive." She shrugged, because it should have ceased to matter years ago.

"What about your mother?"

"I don't remember her. I was three when she died." He squeezed her hand. Molly curled her fingers around his and felt the warmth, the strength.

"Tell me what you know about her," Patrick invited.

There wasn't much. She had been young, just out of high school when Saul married her. He'd been a penniless artist then, but his career had taken off around the time of Molly's first birthday. "She died of one of those influenza epidemics. It was sudden, I guess. Quick. Saul never talks about her. I think he loved her very much." She wanted to believe that, but wasn't sure if it was true.

Patrick's house was looming ahead, a darkening shadow as the moon slipped behind a cloud. Molly felt her heart shift to a slow, heavy beat as they moved closer. Her mouth dried with panic. Inside. She had not been inside his house yet, but she had promised herself to Patrick tonight.

She gulped. "I—Trouble. The cat. I think—I should check on her, shouldn't I?"

"Did you leave her inside?"

She bit her lip. "No. I—no, she went outside just before you picked me up, but I—she——" Patrick's veranda. The steps. She stopped abruptly. Silence. Somewhere, a brush rustled. A deer? Trouble?

Patrick's voice, low and neutral. "I keep finding myself staring at you in the darkness, trying to see what you're thinking. What's wrong, Molly?"

She thought he was coming back down those two steps to her. He didn't. He waited quietly for her to answer, and she realized it wasn't the first time he had done that. He was good at waiting. Good at getting what he wanted, and he wanted her.

She licked her lips. "Patrick, I—I've...never done this before. I—I'm sorry."

He came down those two steps, asked gently, "Sorry for what? For being a virgin?"

For being a hesitant idiot. For not being bolder, going into his arms the way her heart told her to.

He caught her hand and pulled gently. "Come on inside. I'm not going to attack you."

She shouldn't have told him. What a stupid thing to say. If she'd just kept her mouth shut. He would have found out in the end, she supposed, but she could feel the awkwardness between them now, and it was her fault.

There was a light on in the living room, throwing a glow into the small entrance hall. Molly stood in the hall watching Patrick take his overcoat off. "Your turn," he said with faint amusement.

She flushed and fumbled with the zip. He took the jacket from her and led her into the living room. It was paneled inside with cedar, the echo of flames from the fireplace licking warmly along the walls.

She watched as he opened the glass-paned door to the fireplace. His face was flooded with reflections of the red and yellow flames. Would he make love to her on that thick, soft rug in front of the fire?

He might. Then, afterward, they would lie tangled together, close and exhausted with loving. What would it feel like to know she belonged to him in the oldest way of a man and a woman? He would rise to tend the fire and she would watch the warm lights playing over his naked back, heat over the dark heated flesh. She flushed and looked away from him. She'd read too many books, knew nothing of the reality. She should have got some actual practice, because she was such an ignorant fool that the reality was going to be awkward.

"Are you going to sit down?"

She was standing in the middle of his living room. Make yourself comfortable, he'd said as he went to the fire, but she was stuck here like a log. She nodded abruptly now and felt the stiffness of her movements as she walked toward the couch.

The sofa. Long and overstuffed. If she sat there, would he think it an invitation? She gulped and jerked toward the big easy chair that faced the fire. She sat on its edge. He closed the glass door in front of the fire. When he stood up, she felt the tension snap through her like a spring going taut.

He moved to the couch and sat down at one end. Three or four feet between them. She felt silly now, sitting in the chair, a body-language message of hands off. He asked, "Do you want me to take you home, Molly?"

"No," she whispered miserably. She wanted his arms around her. She wanted to be more confident, more experienced.

"Then come here," he commanded gently. "I want you in my arms."

It was the longest three feet she had ever moved across, but he reached out his hand and she put hers in it, then he drew her down beside him and opened his arms and she was shivering as she felt the strong warmth of his shoulder against her cheek.

"Relax, darling," he whispered as he kissed her lips softly, without urgency.

"I'm not sure if I can," she murmured. She could see his smile in the light from the fire. His eyes were dark, gentle on her face. His free hand moved to caress the curling hair away from her face. "It must be a mess," she worried. "My hair."

"Hmm. Wild. Seductive. Tempting. You keep trying to make it look tame and orderly, but it keeps escaping." He bent his head and she felt his breath on her ear, his lips finding their way through the tumble of curls to touch her earlobe with shuddering intimacy.

"I—did you... is the whole house paneled in cedar inside?"

He trapped her chin with his fingers and turned her face so that he could stare down into her eyes. She felt helpless, vulnerable. "Molly, nothing is going to happen here that you don't want to happen."

She swallowed. His eyes traced the movement along her throat.

"You said you didn't want to go home," he reminded her. What was in his voice? Patience. But what was underneath?

"Maybe I should go."

He twisted the curl around his finger again. "I won't stop you, but are you sure it's what you want? You weren't terrified half an hour ago, out under the moon. Do you think I'm going to force you?"

"No." She had never thought that. "It's just—I've never—I might not be... very good."

She looked away, but he filled her vision. His head, his broad shoulders, his arms, surrounding her. She felt completely safe and yet terrified at one and the same time. An impossible mixture of emotions, but real. He carried her hand to the side of his face and she felt her fingers curving against his warm flesh.

"I've known all along, Molly. From the first time I kissed you, I knew there had never been another man. And as for... you couldn't disappoint me." He turned his face into her hand, pressed his lips against her palm.

"I won't hurt you, Molly, and I'll look after you. You know that, don't you?"

Her fingers brushed along the edges of his moustache, the tingling softness along her fingertips. She was in love with him. It was impossible, too soon, but her heart was filled with this man.

"Kiss me," she whispered.

His lips were soft at first, exploring hers, not demanding, but giving. She tried to hold her eyes open, to see the dark heat growing in his gaze, but his lips traveled to her cheek, her eyelids, her temple.

His voice was husky with lazy passion. "I've been dreaming of having you in my arms like this. Kissing you. Your skin soft and heating under my lips." His arm shifted and she felt herself falling back, deeper into his embrace. She could not seem to hold her head up, then his fingers threaded through her hair, sliding along the curls, exploring the shape of her ear, her scalp. His lips sought her throat and she gasped softly as he traced a line of fire from the point of her jaw to the tender hollow at the base of her throat.

He captured her hand and pressed it against his chest. She found the hard thud of his heartbeat, the muscle of his male chest through the soft shirt he wore. She smoothed her palm along the curve of his muscle and felt the sudden hard peak of his small nipple. Then their lips fused again and she threaded her fingers through his hair, feeling the heat rising, explosive as his fingers lightly traced the contours of her breast.

She whimpered when his thumb brushed across the aching tip of her breast through her clothing. When he freed her lips, she turned her face to his throat, her lips seeking blindly against him. She felt his body respond to her caress, heard the ghost of a groan from his lips. Then her lips were seeking through the light dusting of dark hairs where his collar parted and she felt his breathing turning short and ragged.

"Are you trying to drive me mad, Molly?"

"Yes," she whispered, pushing herself away with her hands on his chest, joy and passion welling together. She fumbled with the buttons of his shirt, not quite believing she had the nerve, but driven on by the ragged breathing that told her how her unpracticed caress affected him.

Then his fingers pushed her blouse away and she felt her heart stop beating at his soft groan of wonder. His eyes followed the path of her blouse until it gathered in a silky pool at her elbows, framing the womanly curves that were presented by her lacy bra.

"Molly...so beautiful...darling." His lips sought the warmth of her curves. She found her own arms trapped by her blouse, then somehow it was gone and she felt Patrick's hands fumbling with the clasp of her bra, her own breasts swelling with the aching need to feel his caress.

"Beautiful," he whispered, his hands cupping the swollen curves. She could not breathe. She felt air trying to get inside her lungs, then he lifted her breasts for his kiss and her breath escaped in a harsh groan.

"Molly?" His lips closed over the turgid peak of one swollen breast and her body went limp. She whimpered and threaded her fingers through his hair, holding his mouth close to her aching need. He murmured something. She could not see, could not open her eyes, felt her body arching wildly as his kiss moved from one breast to the other, then to her mouth which had turned sultry and needful.

She pressed up against him, a whimper in her throat as her sensitive nipples found the roughness of his chest pelt. Then his arms tightened and he lifted her. She felt dizziness, heat, half opened her eyes and could see only fire and the glow of desire in black eyes that seemed to devour her hungrily.

Soft roughness against her naked back. She was flat on her back, spread out for his eyes. Above her, his head blocking out the world, the sloping warmth of cedar rising toward the peak of the ceiling above.

The quiet heat before the storm. She stared up and saw all she would ever need in his eyes. She whispered, "When you were tending the fire, I was watching you. I had a fantasy of you making love to me here on this sheepskin rug."

She saw the fire in his eyes, felt her own heartbeat answer. The waiting was heated, full, and she knew that his control would break soon.

"Was it a good fantasy?" he asked in a husky voice filled with loving.

"Yes," she whispered, reaching her fingers to touch the dark shadow of hair that thickened between his male nipples.

"This will be better," he promised as he bent to take her lips with his.

CHAPTER SIX

SHE thought she would die from the sensations. The flames kept surging higher, flooding with responses, with joy and need, then a raging desperation that Molly knew she could not endure.

Her own voice, whimpering, whispering ragged words that were not words at all. Patrick's lips. Heat and loving and need, the explosion echoing closer and closer. A confusion of sounds and sensations. Touch. Caress. Kiss. His lips. Hers. His nipple under her teeth. Her breast drawn inside his mouth.

Her hip thrusting restlessly, finding the hard caress of his hand. Her thighs, sensation, twisting, needing, gasping as his fingers slid closer, caressed the centre of her pulsing need. Sounds. Fire, crawling along her veins as it consumed the wood nearby. Bells somewhere, ringing.

"Please, no..." His voice, low and driven, but when her lips stilled he bent to take her mouth in a deep, consuming kiss that was only a symbol of the joining their bodies hungered for.

The bell. Again. He stilled, lying against her, his breath coming in short, harsh explosions that slowly quietened.

"Patrick...? What——?"

He touched her lips, took her mouth in a slow, tender kiss. "Telephone." His eyes closed painfully as the sound came again. "This time of night, no one would call unless it were important."

He tore himself away from her, all but his eyes which still reflected the flame. He turned away abruptly.

How could she fall in love in two short days? Had she known him in another place, another time, another life? Loved him before, forever? Inevitable, that this one man was the only one for her, that she had waited all her life, not knowing that the emptiness was only a waiting.

In the next room, Patrick's voice changed from question to decision. "No, Sarah, don't wake the kids. I'll be right there. Yes—no, I'll drive you."

Molly found her skirt tangled with Patrick's clothing on the floor. Her blouse was lying in a jumble at the end of the sofa. Patrick was saying patiently, "... know it's almost midnight. Don't worry. I'll call the ferry terminal. They'll have it ready to go for you by the time we get there. Yes, Sarah. I'll call David to come look after the kids. Yes. Five minutes. Bye."

Molly handed Patrick his shirt. He took it in one hand, the other punching out numbers on the telephone. She thought he looked concerned, but not shattered. Not a total disaster, then.

"Thanks," he said, lifting the shirt in a gesture. "My sister," he explained as he waited for an answer to the number he'd dialled. "She's expecting, and it looks as if tonight's the night. Edward's on a trip to Calgary, and—hello? Patrick McNaughton here. We're going to need the ferry for a medical evacuation to Nanaimo, a pregnant woman in labor. Yes, Sarah Hollison. Yes. Yes, that's right, she's calling the doctor right now. I expect he'll meet her at the ferry—no, I'll drive her myself."

As he started dialing again, Molly said quickly, "If you're calling your brother—I'll look after Jeremy and his sister."

He dropped the handset into its cradle and pulled her close for one quick, hard kiss. "Thanks, love. Let's go, then."

She followed him out to his car. "Don't you want to lock your house?" she asked, turning to look back worryingly.

"No need."

She climbed into the passenger seat and Patrick reversed to turn around. As they started along the drive, he covered Molly's hand with his. "Sorry about this, Molly."

Her flesh still tingled from his caresses. She flushed in the darkness and whispered, "It's all right."

"No, it isn't." She glanced and saw a half smile on his lips. "We'll make it up next time," he promised, bringing her hand to his lips.

"Yes," she agreed.

Sarah Hollison was waiting at the door of her house with a small suitcase in her hand. She was a tall woman who would have been slender but for the large swelling of her pregnancy.

"I called the doctor," she told Patrick breathlessly. "He'll meet us at the ferry terminal. I couldn't get Edward on the phone. I—Pat, I can't possibly get into that car. We'd better take my wagon."

"All right," he agreed easily.

"The children——"

"Molly's come to look after them." He reached out to draw her forward.

"The dinosaur lady?" Sarah was doubtful. "Jeremy will be thrilled, but..." Sarah herself obviously was not thrilled about it.

Molly said, "I'll look after them, and if they wake, shall I tell them you've gone to the hospital to have the baby?"

"Oh—yes, do." Sarah gave Molly another doubtful look, but Patrick had the station wagon started and was waiting. "Don't give Sally more than a sip to drink," worried Sarah. "She's been pretty good about wetting her bed, but sometimes ..."

"I won't," promised Molly. "I'll take good care of them. Good luck, Sarah." Who could blame Patrick's sister for being uneasy? All she knew about Molly was that she painted dinosaurs, and that she was the erratic Saul Natham's daughter. Not much of a recommendation for a baby-sitter.

"I'll be glad to get rid of this load," muttered Sarah as she maneuvered her awkward body into the passenger seat.

"I'll phone," Patrick promised.

Molly nodded. "Drive carefully."

"Don't worry." He grinned and indicated Sarah beside him. "With cargo like this, I will."

The world was very quiet when they were gone. Molly started up the stairs to the house, a silhouette throwing a long shadow from the yard light. With her hand on the doorknob, she suddenly turned back and went to Patrick's car. Just as she had suspected, his keys were in the ignition. She supposed it wasn't a Gabriolan sort of thing to do, but she took the keys and locked his car. Then she let herself inside the house.

A notice in the entrance directed guests to the left for registration, straight ahead for dining. Were there guests in residence? No one had mentioned any. Molly moved into the little office where registrations apparently took place, hoping to find a registration book. Nothing. The desk was immaculate, the surface empty except for a gold pen and pencil set. Was April too early in the season for guests? Well, she wasn't about to go looking in drawers. She would worry about guests if any raised their heads or wandered out into the corridor. Her job was the children.

She went up the stairs and found several bedrooms, all open, all empty. Made up for guests, she supposed,

NO RISK, NO OBLIGATION TO BUY...NOW OR EVER!

CASINO JUBILEE
"Scratch'n Match" Game

Here's how to play:

1. Peel off label from front cover. Place it in space provided at right. With a coin, carefully scratch off the silver box. This makes you eligible to receive two or more free books, and possibly another gift, depending upon what is revealed beneath the scratch-off area.

2. You'll receive brand-new Harlequin Presents® novels. When you return this card, we'll rush you the books and gift you qualify for, ABSOLUTELY FREE!

3. Then, if we don't hear from you, every month we'll send you 6 additional novels to read and enjoy, months before they are available in bookstores. You can return them and owe nothing, but if you decide to keep them, you'll pay only $2.24* each plus 25¢ delivery and applicable sales tax, if any*. That's the complete price, and—compared to cover prices of $2.89 each in stores—quite a bargain!

4. When you join the Harlequin Reader Service®, you'll get our subscribers-only newsletter, as well as additional free gifts from time to time, just for being a subscriber!

5. You must be completely satisfied. You may cancel at any time simply by sending us a note or a shipping statement marked ''cancel'' or by returning any shipment to us at our cost.

YOURS FREE!

This lovely heart-shaped box is richly detailed with cut-glass decorations, perfect for holding a precious memento or keepsake—and it's yours absolutely free when you accept our no-risk offer.

CASINO JUBILEE
"Scratch'n Match" Game

**CHECK CLAIM CHART BELOW
FOR YOUR FREE GIFTS!**

YES! I have placed my label from the front cover in the space provided above and scratched off the silver box. Please send me all the gifts for which I qualify. I understand I am under no obligation to purchase any books, as explained on the opposite page.

106 CIH AG5F (U-H-P-02/93)

Name _____

Address _____ Apt. _____

City _____ State _____ Zip _____

CASINO JUBILEE CLAIM CHART

		WORTH 4 FREE BOOKS AND A FREE HEART-SHAPED CURIO BOX
		WORTH 3 FREE BOOKS
		WORTH 2 FREE BOOKS	CLAIM N° 1528

◀ DETACH AND MAIL CARD TODAY! ▶

HARLEQUIN "NO RISK" GUARANTEE

- You're not required to buy a single book—ever!
- You must be completely satisfied or you may cancel at any time simply by sending us a note or a shipping statement marked "cancel" or by returning any shipment to us at our cost. Either way, you will receive no more books; you'll have no obligation to buy.
- The free books and gift you claimed on the "Casino Jubilee" offer remain yours to keep no matter what you decide.

If offer card is missing, please write to: Harlequin Reader Service® P.O. Box 1867, Buffalo, N.Y. 14269-1867

▼ DETACH AND MAIL CARD TODAY! ▼

BUSINESS REPLY MAIL
FIRST CLASS MAIL   PERMIT NO. 717   BUFFALO, NY

POSTAGE WILL BE PAID BY ADDRESSEE

HARLEQUIN READER SERVICE
3010 WALDEN AVE
PO BOX 1867
BUFFALO NY 14240-9952

NO POSTAGE
NECESSARY
IF MAILED
IN THE
UNITED STATES

but vacant now. The children must be downstairs somewhere.

She found them in another section of the big house, back behind the kitchen. This was obviously the private family area, more cluttered than the immaculate rooms in front. Molly followed a vague sound of muttering and found Jeremy's room. He was sleeping in a tumbled mass of bedding, his arms tangled around a pillow, the black hair a messy riot on his head. The muttering seemed to be something about a cave, and a pencil. He was asleep, dreaming, but almost smiling. She smiled too, watching him, feeling tenderness well up.

Sally was sleeping in the next room, her arms and legs tossed out under the blankets in a casual scrawl. She had long, fine blond hair. She must take after her father, decided Molly, tiptoeing out of the girl's room.

Bathroom. Kitchen. Master bedroom. A family room strewn with books and Lego blocks. It must be difficult for Sarah to bend and pick up when she was so largely pregnant. Molly found the box that contained the collection of building blocks and started clearing them up. She was still at it when the telephone rang.

The man at the other end rattled off a number and a question. Molly confirmed. "That's right. You've got the right number." The man obviously hadn't expected a strange voice, so she asked, "Are you Edward Hollison?"

"Yes. I got a message. Who is this? Is Sarah——?"

"She's at the hospital. The baby's coming. Patrick took her on the ferry. Everything's fine."

He seemed stunned, then said worriedly, "Could you get a message to her?" He went into a complex description of the complications of timing airline flights to get home, ending with, "I'll get there as soon as I can. You'll tell Sarah?"

"I'll make sure she gets the message."

"The children——"

"They're fine. Sleeping, and I'm staying here to look after them. I'm Molly, by the way."

"Molly?"

"A neighbor." After Sarah's doubtful reaction, she wasn't about to announce her surname.

"Oh." He sounded confused, probably knew every neighbor in miles, but recovered and said, "Thanks, Molly. We appreciate your help. You'll call the hospital?"

"Right away," she promised, and, after he hung up, she searched through the telephone book, wondering which hospital until she found there was only one.

Only one hospital, but there were over a dozen telephone numbers, everything from radiation to patient information. She decided the information one, dialed and was routed back to a switchboard, but finally received a promise that Mrs. Hollison would get the message as soon as she arrived at the hospital.

Time must have stretched out. They might be on the ferry still. She worried about that for a minute, wondering if Patrick might have to deliver the baby. Sarah could do worse, she thought, because Patrick would be calm and confidence inspiring. Then she remembered that Sarah had said the doctor would be on the ferry as well.

She was dozing in a comfortable easy chair in the family room when the telephone rang again. "Molly? Did I wake you?"

Patrick. She shook her head and said, "Only half. How's Sarah?"

"Now we're here, I think it's going to be a long go." His voice was rueful. "She's fine, but the doctor says don't expect anything before morning. Is everything okay there?"

"Fine. Jeremy's tangled up in a knot of covers. Sally looks like an angel."

He laughed. "She must be sleeping, then. Don't let her fool you. That one can be a real troublemaker. Something like your cat, sweet but tricky. I'm going to be stuck over here until morning, I'm afraid. You sure you're okay?"

"I'm fine." What would he do if she weren't? She decided that he would probably think of something, then remembered and added, "Edward called. Did Sarah get his message?"

"It was waiting for us when we got here. Sarah says thanks, and don't let Jeremy have two sandwiches in his lunch. Apparently he stops off on the way to school and feeds David's chickens. David—so Sarah tells me—is worried about their diet. The chickens' diet, I mean. Not the kids."

Molly curled her legs up and cradled the receiver against her ear, loving that sound of suppressed laughter in his voice, not wanting him to hang up yet. "Is David a worrier?" Would his family ever become her friends? Neighbors, yes, but would Sarah ever smile and offer her coffee and easy talk? Would David frown at her the same way Sarah had?

Patrick said wryly, "David worries more about the cows than the chickens. And Sarah worries about her children."

"Edward, too," said Molly, thinking of his telephone call earlier.

"Hmm." She realized that Patrick didn't want to hang up, either. Strange how intimate it could feel, talking on the telephone. He said, "I'm not sure if Edward worries, or if it's just a habitual way he has of speaking. He has the look, too, his head tilted a bit to one side and his eyes hazy. But I think Sarah does the worrying for both of them."

"What about you, Patrick? Do you worry?" Not a lot, she thought. He would be more inclined to act than to waste time agonizing.

He did not answer, said instead, "*You* do. I'll have to teach you there's no need, Molly. No need to worry."

She didn't know what to say.

"It's going to work, you know." His voice had lost the relaxed ease of a moment ago. "You and I, Molly. We're going to be important to each other. Already are."

She closed her eyes.

"Molly?"

She thought of the doubt in Sarah's eyes, of the way Patrick had believed at first that Molly was one of Saul's lovers. She thought of her upbringing, her life with her roots scattered and shallow. And his. Roots. Family. Deep and secure. It might work for a while, but in the end Patrick McNaughton was bound to realize that Molly Natham did not belong in his world.

"Molly?"

She would take what she could have of his loving. Like Saul, she thought sickly, grasping and losing, seeing the end in the beginning. She licked her lips. "Edward might call again. I'd better hang up, hadn't I?"

She knew he would be frowning, listening to more than her words, trying to see inside. He said. "Consider yourself kissed good night," and she heard the click of the line disconnecting.

Lunches, she thought, getting up, her fingers touching the place where his kiss would have been. Time to think about lunches, not loving.

Sandwiches, Patrick had said. Only one for Jeremy. The kitchen. There was fruit in the refrigerator, and hard-boiled eggs. Celery. She could make cheese celery sticks, two in each lunch, and one sandwich. An apple each. Her hand froze on the fridge door. Tomorrow was Saturday. Surely nobody went to school on Saturday.

Sarah must have forgotten what day it was. No wonder, with the new baby coming. She would be excited, eager, nervous.

What would it be like to have Patrick's child? The thought stirred a trembling sensation in the pit of her stomach. Patrick's children. Hers. They would know they were loved, would always know they could depend on their parents. On her. On Patrick.

"I love him," she whispered, but it was a good thing no one heard because she knew that it would not be as simple as that. If only it could be.

She slept on the couch, woke to the invasion of light through her eyelids. Morning. Quiet. Beside her stood a small worried girl with long, tangled blond hair.

Molly sat up. "Hi. I'm Molly."

Sally looked interested. "The dinosaur lady?"

"That's right. Your mommy's gone to the hospital to have the baby. Are you hungry?"

Sally nodded, still faintly worried but seeing an opportunity here. "Chocolate cake? There's chocolate cake in the fridge."

"No," said Molly, laughing. "Bacon and eggs if you like. Or pancakes. Or cereal."

"Pancakes," decided Sally. "I can eat twenty pancakes. An' Jer'my's hungry, too."

Actually, Sally ate three pancakes. Jeremy ate four, then suggested Molly make a sandwich for him to take outside. Molly said gently, "You're not supposed to feed sandwiches to the chickens. Your Uncle David is afraid it'll make them sick."

"But——"

Sally eyed Molly and announced hopefully, "Chocolate cake is good for snacks, you know. At ten we're supposed to have a snack."

"An apple," said Jeremy, and Sally kicked him under the table.

"Why don't we clean up from breakfast?" suggested Molly. "Then we could go over to my place and see how the cat's doing."

Sally also seemed to have a firm relationship with Trouble, and she quickly agreed to the plan. At the cabin, Molly changed into jeans and a sweatshirt, more appropriate for baby-sitting than her long pleated skirt and silky blouse. The blouse was already stained with a few drops of sticky syrup from breakfast.

"Can we get the mail?" asked Sally as Molly locked the cabin.

"Sally always wants to get mail," said Jeremy. "She likes the advertising pictures."

"I've got a scrapbook," Sally explained. "But there might be letters for you in the box, so you'd want to go, wouldn't you, Molly?"

"I don't know where the mail comes," said Molly as she dropped the keys into the front pocket of her jeans.

"At the site," said Jeremy. "We'll show you."

"Mr. Natham's got box seven," Sally volunteered. "And the key is that little one on your keys. I saw him get mail lots of times. Can we go? It's only a couple of telephone poles down the road!"

Molly had expected she would have to go to the post office to figure out the mail problem, but Jeremy and Sally were quite certain, leading the way, running ahead.

Not surprisingly, when Molly opened the rural post box she found an impressive pile of window envelopes addressed to Saul. Bills, and probably in arrears, knowing her father. The next time he called, she would ask where to send them. Easier to pay them herself, Molly decided. He had given her the cabin, a birthday present, and so what if it had a few little strings attached? Tomorrow, she would sit down and write out some checks.

On the way back, Molly and the children were overtaken by a battered truck driven by a man wearing a baseball cap. David McNaughton, older than Patrick, but recognizably his brother. He parked the truck and climbed out, a weather-beaten man, dressed for farm work in ancient jeans and a matching jacket. His face was harsh, his manner abrupt but not unfriendly.

"Pat called," he announced. "You'll be Molly. I came over to tell you supper at my place tonight. Pat's stuck at the hospital until Ed gets there, and with the fog lying in the harbor the flights are all stalled. Pat'll be along when he can. Sarah's taking her time, he says." He looked at the two children with an affectionate scowl. "I can take them off your hands."

She shook her head. "I'm enjoying them, but supper sounds great. What can we bring? There's a chocolate cake, and I could make some salad."

"I thought we'd never get to eat the cake," Sally whispered to Jeremy.

They had just begun to eat their supper when Patrick arrived at the farm that evening.

"Grab a plate," called David as Patrick closed the door behind himself. Molly started to get up, but David snapped, "Sit down, Molly. Pat's not helpless."

"Better do as he says," warned Patrick with a laugh. "My brother's a tyrant, and he doesn't like to be crossed."

"Darned right, I don't, but that never stopped my kid brother. Now go get your own plate. Molly's been busy enough with these hooligans."

Sally and Jeremy giggled and Patrick disappeared into the kitchen, calling back, "We're uncles again, Dave!"

"Boy or girl?"

"Boy." His voice was muffled in the clatter of utensils, then he was back with an empty plate and a glass of milk. He smiled at them all and sought out Molly with his eyes. "And a girl," he added, sitting down at the empty place across from Molly. "Which serves Sarah right for refusing to have that scan done. She'll have to buy a whole new set of baby things. Pass the meat, please, Jeremy."

"Twins?" David was amused, too.

Patrick explained to Molly as he shifted two slices of roast beef on to his plate, "Sarah's dead against any medical procedure she doesn't think is necessary, and a while back when the doctor admitted everything seemed okay Sarah refused to have an ultrasound scan—otherwise she'd have known it was twins."

Jeremy wailed, "But, Uncle Pat, if it's a boy *and* a girl, who wins our bet? If it's a boy I get to go to the PNE in August, but if it's a girl——"

"We both won, so you get to work on the wood pile and I'll get the tickets," Patrick added with a laugh, "Edward's stunned. He arrived around five, just after the big event. Incidentally, Molly, he's staying over in Nanaimo tonight. I said you'd not mind staying another night, but I can stay just as easily."

"They can come here," offered David.

Molly shook her head. "I can stay. I don't mind."

"Just call us if they give any trouble," said Patrick, shaking his head at Jeremy's yell of outrage at the suggestion. "Be good for Molly," he warned, "or you can forget the PNE. Now pass the potatoes. I'm starving."

After supper, David refused Molly's offer to help with the dishes. "Pat and I will do them. Go relax in the living room."

It was a sprawling, comfortable room.

As soon as Molly sat down, Jeremy found a piece of paper and a pencil and asked Molly to draw dinosaurs for them. She obliged, adding all sorts of unlikely creatures to the drawing as Sally kept coming up with wilder and wilder ideas. Patrick joined them and suggested a goose and an eagle; then David came in, looked over Jeremy's shoulder and commented that cows had shorter legs than that.

"I haven't studied cows," Molly defended herself, laughing.

Later, Patrick drove them back to the Hollisons' home in the station wagon, coming inside to help Molly settle the children into bed.

Our children, she thought, and she was beginning to believe that one day it might be. He took her hand and led her out of Sally's bedroom, whispering, "Penny for your thoughts."

She smiled. "That I'm glad Saul gave me the cabin. And that I like your family."

He drew her into the family room, then into his arms. "Only my family? Kiss me, Molly. I've been aching for that ever since I left you last night."

He kissed warmly, his lips firm and gently demanding. "I'm not staying," he told her, his breath hot against her cheek, her ear. "I'm not making love to you for the first time in my sister's house, with my niece and nephew bursting in in the middle."

She drew his head down, opened her lips to welcome his and whispered, "Stay for just a minute more."

"You're a wild temptress," he growled, taking what she offered.

"Is that good?"

"You're good." He slid his hands intimately along her body, leaving her gasping when he abruptly moved away, saying roughly, "We're good."

"Patrick——"

"You're playing with fire, Molly. High explosives. I'm getting out of here while I can. Call me if you need anything." His eyes seared into hers and she knew that he was right. If he stayed any longer...

She watched the taillights of his car fading away down the drive, watched until she heard a sound from behind and had to turn to tend to Sally, who wanted a big drink of water. Remembering Sarah's concerns about bed-wetting, Molly gave her a small sip, then put her to bed and read her three pages of *Bronty Goes to Hawaii*, by which time Sally was soundly asleep.

Molly went out to the kitchen to clean up from the children's bedtime snack. Her hand went to her own flat abdomen, thinking of children and babies. Of Patrick. She bit her lip, knowing she was building dream castles with no foundation. Patrick wanted a relationship, yes, but that was a long way from children and forever. He was a man in his mid-thirties, a man who had never married. There was no reason to think that would change simply because his voice went husky when they were close. He wanted her. He liked her, too, but he might have felt the same for dozens of other women. Us, he had said, but she wasn't naive enough to believe that meant forever.

But her heart pounded thick in her veins when the telephone rang. She knew it would be Patrick.

"I called to say good night." His voice was warm and if she closed her eyes she could see him.

"You already said it. You were right. Sally woke up."

"I figured she would. It's a nightly routine. Do you dance?"

"Yes. Why?"

"I'm going to take you dancing when this is over, when Edward gets home to look after his own kids at night. Not on the island," he added with a laugh.

She smiled, remembering the group that had descended on them in the White Hart.

"Do you know what I want to do with you, Molly?" He heard her soft intake of breath and said huskily,

"Think about all the ways I want to touch you. Dream about me, Molly."

He hung up, leaving her with the dial tone in her ear and the memory of his voice. She felt the warm excitement that seemed to have become a permanent part of her since she met him.

She went up to look for a bed for herself. She needed a proper sleep tonight. These bedrooms were all made up and ready for guests, but they were too far away from the children. In the end she took a duvet from one of the guest beds and brought it down to the couch in the family room. No guests due for two weeks, Jeremy had said earlier, so she didn't have to worry about being called upon to run a bed and breakfast. She'd never even stayed in one.

She had expected to drift off with the memory of Patrick's voice in her ears, but her brain was churning with activity. She tossed from one side to the other, thinking of Patrick alone in the house next door, of her cabin lying empty, of Saul somewhere far away and Babette talking about smuggling.

The couch was too narrow for restlessness. Molly finally got up and made herself a cup of instant cocoa in the kitchen, then went to look in on the children.

Sally was sleeping, angelic and sprawled all over the bed. Jeremy was tangled in the sheets again, his dark curly hair wild around his head. Would Patrick's children have that curly dark hair and those black eyes? They would have to be dark, with Molly and Patrick for parents.

"Stop it," she whispered to herself in agony. If she went on like this, she would end by begging Patrick to love her forever, clinging and turning his affection to irritation. Molly knew the rules, had learned long ago that nothing destroyed love as quickly as asking for more.

Don't ask. Don't want. Welcome what comes, but never ask for more.

Saul's mail, she thought, desperate for something other than Patrick to occupy her mind. She would look through it, find out if anyone had got to the point of foreclosing on her father. And she would pay the bills. Not just because he'd been so generous with the house, but also because she didn't want the power or telephone cut off. She supposed she would have to go around eventually and change things over into her name. Meanwhile, she would pay Saul's utility bills and use his services.

She took the stack of mail to the kitchen table and started opening bills, using a table knife for a letter opener. The telephone company had sent an overdue notice, and a current statement with several calls to Europe on it. Five hundred dollars! She would have to transfer some money from her savings to pay that one.

The electricity was a month overdue, too, but it wasn't as bad as the telephone. Molly put aside an envelope addressed in fine, rounded handwriting. Female handwriting. She would send it on when she had Saul's address.

The library at Malaspina College was demanding the return of four books with fines of forty-three dollars accumulated to date. Molly would have to look for the books. If they weren't in the cabin, she didn't hold out a lot of hope of getting Saul to send them back.

The next envelope was a familiar blue color. She slit it open and began to slide the statement out; then stopped when she recognized the form and colors. Revenue Canada. She smiled and put it aside without reading it. Telephone and hydro-electricity were fine, but she drew the line at paying Saul's taxes.

The next thing she opened was a bill from a courier company. He must have shipped paintings somewhere.

Four months ago, she saw from the statement. That would have been from his last showing in Toronto.

She sorted the piles. Statements to be paid. The letter and the Revenue Canada thing to be forwarded when she had an address. Taxes. Had he paid the taxes on the Gabriola property and the cabin? She frowned, trying to remember whether there had been anything about that in the papers from the lawyer. Tomorrow she would check for sure.

Had Saul paid the lawyer? She shook that off. Utilities, that was as far as she was willing to go. And the courier, she decided, adding that to the utility statements. Her eyes fell on the blue envelope again and she wondered if she was misjudging Saul. He had obviously become more efficient about paperwork since her childhood. To get his tax assessment in April, he must have filed his return back in January. Three months earlier than required.

She shook her head. Three months early? Saul? That was so unlikely as to be virtually impossible. More likely late, she thought. It might not be a statement at all, but a demand of some sort for a delinquent return. In that case, she had better know so she could tell him when he called again.

It wasn't an assessment, she realized as she unfolded it again. At least, it was not the original assessment. It was one of the statements they sent out, balance due and interest on deficient installment payments. She'd had them herself, because it was almost impossible for her to guess her proper installment payments ahead when her royalties varied so much.

So Saul must have——

Her statements had never had penalties added on. The electricity and the telephone weren't the only people Saul had kept waiting. This particular creditor had placed a

very specific threat on the bottom of the bill. Pay, or
have everything you owned seized.

Only Saul would be crazy enough to forget to pay his
taxes. She would have to pay this, too. She'd better go
to Nanaimo on Monday, find a branch of her bank and
pay this thing, because the deadline on the statement
was only a few days away. If it didn't get paid, the bailiff
would be after Saul and his worldly possessions.

They would come looking at his last known address
first. Official cars, official people demanding to know
where Saul Natham was. She could not answer that
question. How could he be so stupid as to neglect his
tax bill?

Molly smoothed the statement and looked at the details of what was owing. This had been going on a while.
Interest and penalties. Legal fees? That sounded
ominous. The total...

Surely that total was wrong.

Then she remembered Babette saying gleefully what
fun it was to be a fugitive. Molly had thought it was
some crazy joke. Now she knew better.

CHAPTER SEVEN

AMAZING how easy it was to avoid Patrick when she set her mind to it. He knew. Every so often she would catch his eyes on her, as if he was biding his time.

Molly could feel the ominous pressure building up as the days crawled past. Waiting for the other shoe to drop, she thought wildly. So much like the days of ramshackle wandering with Saul. At the age of eleven she had known how to act as a buffer between the looming creditors and her father, how to negotiate two more weeks in rooms with rent in arrears.

Never again, she had vowed when Aunt Carla had rescued her from all that. Molly would stay out of trouble, play every game by the rules. Keeping out of trouble meant, of necessity, keeping out of her father's tangled life. That might have been difficult, because Molly loved her father deeply, but Saul's own wandering life-style had protected her once she went to live with her aunt and uncle.

Their contacts over the last fourteen years had consisted of Saul's unexpected visits, occasional offhand gifts, and Molly's reading about her father's successes in art magazines. Once, she had attended an exhibition of his paintings in Toronto, had seen him across the room in a tangle of people. A year later he had telephoned her from Bolivia. She had no idea where he had been in between.

Aunt Carla had warned her. Any gift from Saul was going to have strings attached. Molly shivered, staring at the dinosaur taking shape on the canvas in front of her. Why had she let Saul hand her another dream with a catch? After all these years. As if she were still a gullible kid.

Patrick. He was waiting, watching. Patient, but he would not let her avoid him forever. She hated the thought of the end, official men in official cars, asking questions and the news flying everywhere. She was living in Saul's last known address, and they would come. Then everyone would know. Molly was a newcomer, but she had overheard the easy gossip that flew. Natural, in such a small community.

"Molly Natham? You know, that artist's kid. The one who's up for tax evasion. Yes, off somewhere in Europe, and I saw the sheriff up on McNaughton Road yesterday, and the daughter was..."

Patrick was an honorable man, honest, and tax evasion was no joke. Molly supposed it would be easier if she packed her van and drove away. Perhaps she would, when Sarah was back home; although running from awkward situations was Saul's game, another pattern she had vowed not to repeat. Meanwhile, she blessed Sarah's hospital stay, because otherwise there would be no Hollison children to keep Molly busy.

Sarah's husband Edward turned up on Sunday morning, looking tired and faintly worried. Molly sent him off to bed to get some rest. She could look after the children.

On Monday morning, Jeremy and Sally went off to catch their school bus with lunches Molly had packed. Patrick called to say he was off to Nanaimo, but would see her that evening.

"Have a good day," she said to Patrick, neither agreeing or disagreeing about that evening.

She cleaned the Hollison house, then slipped over to her own cabin for three hours with the dinosaurs. By the time Patrick got back from his offices in Nanaimo at five-thirty, Molly was back at the Hollisons', cooking supper and answering a million questions from Sally about where was Ottawa and did they really have the gover'ment there for all Canada?

Patrick frowned at the salad and said, "I didn't intend to turn you into a maid, Molly. I'll talk to Edward. We'll get someone in to take over here."

She turned away to get the tomatoes from the crisper. "I don't mind it." She was not ready to be alone with Patrick yet, she thought desperately. Perhaps Saul would call. Maybe she could talk him into straightening out this mess. Then she and Patrick could...

"Molly, this is too much. You've got your own work to do."

"It's all right," she insisted. "Jeremy and Sally go to school. Today I went to the cabin and worked most of the day on dinosaurs."

Mercifully, he let it pass.

On Tuesday, Molly made a quick trip into Nanaimo, going to a branch of her bank to transfer funds so she could pay Saul's bills. Paying her father's European telephone calls certainly put a hole in her savings, but five hundred dollars was nothing to that other massive threat. She checked the balance of her own accounts, but no magic was going to turn a small nest egg into an extra two hundred thousand dollars to pay Saul's tax bill.

On Wednesday she learned that Sarah had a slight infection and was being kept in hospital with the babies for a few days more. Not serious, Edward told her, although he himself seemed worried. When Patrick heard about Sarah's extended hospital stay, he renewed his suggestion that he hire help for Molly.

"Or I'll take a few days off work myself and help you out," he decided, although Molly knew that he had an important deadline on a major consultation.

Edward decided, "We'll hire someone," and Molly found herself talking to him, which was easier than meeting Patrick's eyes.

"I'm really enjoying it, Edward," she insisted. "I'd be disappointed if you got someone else."

She was still sleeping at the Hollisons'. Easier for looking after the children's breakfast, she told Patrick. In between the meals and the children and avoiding being alone with Patrick, Molly was pursuing a fierce telephone search for Saul. She knew it was foolish to think talking would change anything, but she had to try. She had found Saul's address book stuffed into a bookcase upstairs in the cabin. Alone in the cabin during the days, she was working her way through the telephone numbers in the black book.

Futile. A woman in New York told Molly she had heard Saul was living somewhere on Vancouver Island...Saul's agent hadn't heard from the artist in two months, obviously wasn't about to tell Molly anything even if he had...a California number rang endlessly with no answer.

Friday was the deadline on the notice from Revenue Canada. Molly spent the day walking around in a state of near panic, accomplishing nothing. How long did she have before the sky fell on her? If she got through Friday without disaster appearing, she would be safe until Monday morning.

She called numbers in Vancouver, San Diego and Tijuana, spending most of the day trying to get through to the Mexican number and facing a stream of incomprehensible Spanish when she succeeded.

Nobody admitted to knowing where her father was.

Babette's number was in there, in the "P"'s. The blonde had an answering machine. Molly had left messages on it every day since Wednesday.

Friday, and the weekend was looming with its own problems. Patrick, and sooner or later they would be alone. If only she could find Saul first!

Molly was sleeping in her own bed now, although she supposed it was really the government's bed. She had once read a book on business law and she was pretty sure it was illegal to transfer property for the purpose of avoiding a debt. There wasn't much doubt that Saul had given the cabin to Molly to avoid letting the government have it. That meant the transfer wasn't legal and could be canceled by the court. And even if that didn't happen she would have to give up the ·cabin. Morally, it belonged to the government in settlement of the overdue taxes.

She was living here on borrowed time. Neither the government, nor Patrick, would wait forever to claim what was theirs. One of these nights Patrick was going to come knocking on her door. She thought he would wait until Sarah was back home. He knew that Molly was going short of sleep, staying late at the Hollisons' each night so that Edward could visit Sarah in Nanaimo.

On Sunday, Patrick turned up at the Hollisons' just as Molly was serving lunch to Edward and the children.

"Had lunch?" asked Edward.

"Thanks. I've eaten." Molly recognized the determined look on his face, wasn't surprised when he announced, "I'm taking Molly out for the afternoon. She needs a break. Ed, you'll be okay?"

"I'd planned to visit Sarah and the twins this afternoon."

Patrick nodded. He had already allowed for that. "David's expecting the kids. Just drop them off on your way to the ferry. Molly, are you ready?"

She looked around desperately. "I've got to do the dishes."

"Can we come?" demanded Sally. "We need a break, too, Uncle Pat."

Patrick shook his head. "This break is just for Molly." His voice wasn't allowing any argument.

"Go ahead, Molly," said Edward. "Enjoy yourself. You've earned it."

She felt more like a lamb going to the slaughter than a woman going out with the man she loved. What could she say? Patrick, my father's about to be charged with tax evasion? However Patrick might react to that, Molly simply did not have the nerve to say the words. Perhaps it was not only a lack of courage, but also the habit of a lifetime of keeping her problems to herself.

"Where are we going?" she asked. She wished she could hide her head in the sand, enjoy what he had to give her, and pretend tomorrow wasn't going to come.

Patrick, concentrating on the winding North Road, answered idly, "Originally, I thought of a walk to the petroglyphs."

"The *what*?"

He smiled. "So you are listening. I thought you were a few thousand miles away."

Probably she had been. As far away as France or Belgium. Wherever it was her father had decided to hide out, it was bound to be a long way from here.

"What are petro—whatsits?"

"Petroglyphs. Rock carvings made by the native Indians of this area. They've been found here and there on the exposed rock surfaces of Gabriola. There are some about half a mile back behind your place."

"In the middle of the bushes?" She stared at the road ahead. Half a mile? "But we're not going there?" She felt his shrug and turned to look at him. His face was almost grim, more like David's harsh features than the Patrick she was growing to know.

He said flatly, "The way you've been avoiding me lately, I suspect you'd run for your life if I took you off alone into the bushes."

She swallowed sudden dryness in her throat. "So—so where *are* we going?"

"Victoria."

Coward! Why couldn't she ask him to turn back, to take her to see the rock carvings, anywhere that he would take her in his arms and make her forget.

"What are you worrying about, Molly?"

"Worrying?" She supposed that he could read it in her. Even at the beginning, he had seemed able to see right through her defenses.

"Your eyes," he said quietly, keeping *his* eyes on the road, which didn't seem to stop him reading her mind. "And you're not eating. You're feeding everyone else, but pushing your own food around the plate. Damn it, Molly! In the last week, you've got visibly thinner!" He pulled the car into the right lane as he passed a junction, then came to a smooth stop behind a pickup truck. The ferry lineup. Ahead, the ferry was just docking. Patrick turned the key off, then Molly heard the emergency brake go on. He turned toward her, his hand resting on the back of her seat, not quite touching.

"Are you going to tell me what's worrying you?"

She bit her lip. Patrick was accustomed to solving problems. Sarah called him when she needed help. Jeremy and Sally were in the habit of dropping over and telling him their problems. The other day at the farm, Molly had heard David talking to Patrick about a mysterious problem he was having with the cows. One had died and two others were behaving strangely.

It was not only family who turned to Patrick when they had problems. A group of professionals wanted him to run for political office, thought he could help solve the province's problems.

Even Trouble had chosen Patrick's walls to climb when Saul abandoned her.

"Molly?"

She stared at the little stream of cars coming off the ferry. Sunday afternoon, light traffic. Soon he would have to start the Corvette and drive on. She watched the last car drive toward them, then a single foot passenger walked along the ramp on to the ferry. Patrick started his engine and released the emergency brake just as the man standing on the side of the loading ramp waved the line of vehicles to come forward.

On the ferry, he turned off the key and set the emergency brake, then said abruptly, "Let's go outside."

She followed him to the front of the ferry and leaned against the rail beside him, looking down at the water. A shadow moved over the water and she looked up to find the eagle circling lazily high overhead. She thought of asking Patrick again where he was taking her, where in Victoria, or why, but it did not matter. She would go anywhere he asked. She had known that almost from the first.

"Are you angry with me about something?"

She shook her head mutely.

"I didn't think you were, but..."

She hugged her jacket closer. He would know soon enough. He might believe she had known about the tax thing all along, had helped Saul evade the authorities.

He said quietly, "I want to help. Whatever it is that's got you so worried, Molly, I want to help you."

Of course he would. She bit her lip, then released it when she realized he was watching, adding up information. With those eyes, he might actually guess. 'I—— It's just...'' She tried desperately to think of some excuse for her behavior. She was worried about her work? Sure. Couldn't eat because a dinosaur was giving her a hard time. She cleared her throat to stop the hysterical laughter that threatened to rise up. "Look, I..."

"Are you short of money?" She shook her head and his frown deepened. "You're not sick? Some medical——"

"No! I——". She closed her eyes, said harshly, "Please, Patrick? I need some—some space. Could you back off?" When she found the courage to meet his eyes, he was studying her grimly.

He said, "I'm glad you decided not to lie about whatever it is."

So he knew that she had been trying to dream up some fictitious excuse for her behavior. "You're psychic," she muttered. "I—I wouldn't lie to you."

"Good." He draped an arm around shoulders, drawing her against him. "Now why don't you try relaxing? Enjoy being a tourist. No worries. No hassles. A day of escape."

"Escape from everything?" Escape was impossible. She knew that, but the idea was tempting.

"Everything," he promised, then he kissed her lightly and somehow it seemed possible to escape for one day of fantasy.

She had never been to the old Victorian city that was British Columbia's provincial capital. It reminded her a bit of Ottawa, especially the old legislative buildings. "All lit up at night," Patrick told her. "Outlined in lights. It's quite a sight." After the legislature lawns, he took her to a newsstand and searched for a big postcard to show her the magical nighttime outline.

"I'll send it to Aunt Carla and Uncle Gordon."

He had a booklet of stamps in his wallet and she wrote the postcard out right there, then they found a postbox and she laughed, saying, "You don't believe in putting things off, do you."

"Not if it can be avoided," he agreed, and took her hand to lead her to a horse-drawn carriage parked at the side of the road. "Ever been on a horse-and-carriage tour?" he asked.

"Never with you," she answered, and it was magical. In the back of the carriage, Patrick settled her in the curve of his arm and she knew that was where she belonged. Even Saul could not take this day from her. It was springtime. The old port of Victoria was in bloom, flowers everywhere, tourists laughing and talking, shooting pictures of everything from the famous Butchart gardens to the Royal Victoria Wax Museum.

From the wax museum, Patrick was going to take her to the undersea gardens; but when she said her feet were sore he took her instead down to the Causeway, a walk along the harbor's edge. There were sailing ships, tall masts against the blue harbor and the clear sky. There was also a ragged man with a guitar singing songs for coins.

Patrick added to the coins, then sat down on one of the wide concrete steps with Molly to listen to the love song. When he kissed her, very gently, very softly, the music was everywhere.

"I wish this day would go on forever," she whispered.

"It isn't over yet. Dinner next. Seafood, I think."

"Nowhere fancy, I hope? You dragged me off in my blue jeans." She wasn't worried, really, because Patrick was wearing a pair of black corduroy trousers and a casual blue shirt with a V-neck sweater over it. Sexy, she thought whenever her eyes fell on the way the sweater clung to his broad shoulders.

"A low-class joint," he promised, but he took her to a quiet dining room filled with a mixture of everything from tattered jeans to evening dress. They ate scallops and drank wine. Patrick toasted her new dinosaur book.

Molly forced herself to toast his career in politics. Inflicting pain on herself.

She smiled brightly at him and asked, "Did you say yes to Gary and his cronies? Next Friday, you told them, and next Friday's gone."

"Hmm." He had her hand in his, was playing absently with her fingers. "They gave me a respite. The MLA who was about to step down has changed his mind. I'm off the hook for the moment."

"But you *will* do it? In the end you'll do it?" She wanted him to say no. It might be possible for her to have a future with a Patrick who had a private life. Saul's disasters might not matter too much.

At least—*did* Patrick want a future with her? An affair, yes. But...

"Maybe I will," he said slowly. "The next provincial election isn't for a year. No hurry to decide."

For a man like Patrick, solving problems for the province was just one more step in the natural progression. "I can see you in those parliament buildings." She lifted her glass with determination. "You might end up prime minister."

He laughed, but it was no joke. He took her hand and she curled her fingers around it, tightly.

"Do you see yourself in that crystal ball," he asked. "Standing beside me?"

In dreams, not in real life. She took her hand away and said in a shaken voice, "I can't see the future," and hoped it was true.

"Dance with me, Molly."

She had been watching the few couples who were brave enough to try dancing on the tiny space between tables. There was a band, making music, and conversation all around, drowning out the singer, who was wailing something about a train that kept on rolling.

Patrick put his arms around her, moving to the faintly heard drum of music. Molly closed her eyes and let her cheek settle against the soft wool that covered his shoulder. Escape, he had promised her. One day might be all she had before the bailiffs turned up. She let her arms slide up around his neck. The irresistible force, she thought. And she was no immovable object.

"I like it when you smile like that." His whisper tickled her ear. "It makes me think of secrets whispered, of loving." He turned them to avoid collision with another couple and his arms tightened. "I love you, Molly. You know that, don't you?"

Oh, God! She squeezed her eyes tightly closed. *Please!* she begged silently. No tears! She must *not* cry!

The tempo of the music changed. Faster. Wilder. She slipped out of his arms, moving to the music, his eyes holding hers. She had no right to trap him with her own words of love, not when her life contained a tangle that could easily destroy his future.

A year, he had said. A year until the next election. Was that long enough for Saul's fugitive status to be forgotten? Saul, damn him, had made headlines all his life.

Patrick caught her close against him as the music slid back to a slow, seductive beat. "Let's get out of here," he whispered. "I'm taking you home."

Whose home? His? Or her temporary haven, the cabin that might actually be evidence in a tax evasion case? Saul, who had more than once claimed loudly that taxes were forced payment for services he had not asked society to provide.

"One more dance," Molly begged, going into his arms and knowing he would not refuse her. With that look in his eyes, she thought he might give her anything, this man who said he loved her.

Somehow she must find the strength not to ask for more than this one day of escape. Strong arms. She loved his strength. She moved her cheek on his shoulder and felt his hands settle just above her hips as he moved slowly to the music. She wanted forever in his arms.

"Can we go for another carriage ride?" she asked shakily.

In darkness, they glided along the waterfront behind the clopping hooves of the horse. Molly closed her eyes and breathed in the musky scent of the man she loved.

"Look, or you'll miss it," he teased her softly, and when she opened her eyes the magical castle was there, an outline of the old buildings in lights against the night sky.

"Magic," she breathed. "I believe in magic."

"Sure you do." A smile in his voice. "And dinosaurs who get lost in big cities, with saviors to come rescue them." He bent his lips to her ear and whispered, "You make me believe in magic."

She closed her eyes on painful sweetness, said in a shaken voice, "I like fantasy. It has neat endings, happy endings."

"So does life, if you take happiness when it offers." He took her chin gently in his hand, turned her face up to his. "You love me, don't you, Molly?"

Better if she could lie. She curled her fingers into the softness of his sweater. "I—I shouldn't. Patrick, it can't work, you and I—there's——" Nothing she could explain to him.

"Why not?"

"I——" She gulped and reached desperately for a distraction. "The children—I should be back there to look after them."

"They're staying at David's tonight."

She had known, really, that Patrick had arranged something for them. Otherwise, he would have had her back much earlier. The carriage stopped at an intersection. Molly wanted to pull his head down, his lips to hers. He was holding himself back, keeping his desires in control for her sake. He wanted her, could easily have swept her into passion with just one of those shattering kisses. But he knew something was wrong.

He had no right to be so understanding, willing to wait for her to explain. If he would get angry with her erratic behavior it would all be easier. Angry, then over.

Or if he would kiss her, really kiss her.

A silent voice taunted her. Taking responsibility out of your hands, Molly? Seducing you? Later, would she look back and say the man had tempted her, swept her off her feet? If she hadn't the courage to tell him the truth about Saul and his gift, at least she could be honest about this. She curled her fingers tighter into Patrick's sweater, brought her lips to his.

"I don't want to go back," she whispered, knowing that going back, crossing the harbor in that ferry, she would feel that sense of impending disaster crawling back over her. He took her lips, her mouth, but she could feel the passion still leashed in him.

"What is it you want?" he demanded. "To ride behind a horse all night, looking at city lights?"

She closed her eyes, but knew she would give him truth as far as she could. "Escape," she admitted. "That's what I want. I've never done this, skipped off and not come home all night. I knew girls who did in school, but I was always afraid to."

He was amused. "There's no one back on Gabriola keeping track of your movements. You're a big girl now."

She swallowed and whispered, "Please. Isn't there somewhere we could...stay? Here in Victoria. Tonight."

His hands took her face and turned it so he could study her in the reflection from the street lights. His mouth was a hard line, his eyes dark and narrowed.

"If I stay with you tonight, Molly, I'm going to want to make love with you."

She touched her lower lip with her tongue. "I want that too."

She felt the shudder go through him. Then he leaned forward to speak quietly to the driver. "Are you crazy?" she whispered when he took her back in his arms after the horse had turned in the direction Patrick had requested. "That's a luxury hotel. I saw it when we went past. Have you forgotten how I'm dressed?"

His hand slid down along her jacket to the denim-clad firmness of her hip. "I've been noticing all day. I like you in jeans, especially when they're a little tight here," he decided, sliding his hand suggestively under cover of darkness.

She gasped. "The hotel—— They'll expect luggage and——"

"A gold credit card will look after it."

"I didn't know you were a cynic."

"Occasionally."

In the hotel, the porter showed Molly and Patrick to the luxury suite with smooth hospitality. Inside the room, Patrick picked up a telephone and made a quiet list of requests.

"I'm impressed," breathed Molly when the soft knock came on the door a few minutes later. A cart with champagne and glasses was quietly rolled in, while another attendant slipped into the bathroom to lay out razor, shaving cream and toothbrushes. Molly giggled when they were alone again. "I'd never have the nerve to ask for toothbrushes in a hotel."

Patrick poured a glass of the champagne and pressed it into her hand. "You don't have to be nervous, Molly." She gasped and he said, "Your eyes. They change color with the beat of your heart." He threaded the fingers of one hand through her hair.

"It needs brushing after that wind," she said breathlessly.

"I want to kiss you."

"I'll drop my glass." Her fingers curled around it. "And I'll melt."

He moved away from her, then the lights were gone. All that was left was the glow from the harbor lights coming through the window, and the shadow of her lover as he came back across the room.

He took her glass away and slid the jacket off her shoulders. It dropped to the floor and he said, "There's no ice in you. How could you melt?"

Easily, she thought as she felt his light touch on her shoulder. "You're beautiful," he whispered.

"In a sweatshirt and jeans?" She might have laughed, but she could hardly breathe. "I wish you'd let me change before you took me out. I would have worn something pretty. Something..."

"I was afraid to," he admitted. "I was afraid you'd shut the door of your cabin and keep me out."

He must have done something to the panel on the wall, because there was music, soft and languorous. He caressed her hair, untangling it, drawing it away from her face. She could hear her own breathing, his.

"I won't hurt you," he promised. "And I'll protect you."

She confessed, "I've been aching, dreaming you." Loving him, but she sealed the word behind her lips.

His lips were slow on hers, teasing, not taking. Brushing her full lower lip, waiting, feeling her response. He moved to caress her cheek, her eyes, her temple where a pulse beat thick and heavy.

When her hands sought restlessly in the soft thickness of his sweater, he drew them away and pulled the sweater off with a smooth motion. The music was a pulse, beating around them. Anticipation. She could feel the hard ridges of his chest muscles through the shirt, the soft areas where his hair grew thickly. She groaned when the open palms of his hands brushed slowly across the peaks of her breasts.

She wasn't aware of undoing the buttons of his shirt until she felt her fingers searching through the tight dark hairs that grew underneath. Then her arms were tangled in her own sweatshirt as he drew it away and threw it back somewhere, to join his sweater.

"Are you going to kiss me?" Was that her voice? That husky, seductive breath?

His voice was slow, husky, promising, "I'm going to love you." She felt the muscles go tight at the pit of her stomach as his hands shaped the upper slopes of her breasts above her bra. "Slowly," he said harshly. "As slowly as I can."

Her fingers curled around the hard bulge of his male chest, fondling the tangle of his hair as he moved close to her. He bent to trace the curve of her breast with his lips. Her legs turned to rubber as a heavy pulse beat at her center.

"I told you I'd melt," she said raggedly.

His answer was a low growl. He released her, but only for a moment, his fingers trembling as they freed the fastener of her jeans. He left the denim covering behind as he swung her into his arms.

She had thought she would be shy, lying almost naked on the massive bed with Patrick staring down at her white flesh in the moonlight. She was better covered than she would be in a bikini, but she had always been a girl for one-piece bathing suits. And shy, until tonight.

"Beautiful," he whispered.

He was so careful with her, holding his own passion tightly leashed. Then, abruptly, there was only need and the harsh gasp in his throat when she moved against him. And fire.

His hands, caressing away the silky scraps of fabric that separated them. His lips, teasing the turgid swelling of her breasts, then drawing her need deeply inside his mouth, driving her so wild that her fingers curled hard into the muscles at his shoulders, her teeth worried the firm flesh of his shoulder.

His hand, probing her restlessness, finding her moist and heated with woman's passion. Careful, so careful, invading the place that was only his. Hard, needing, holding back until she felt the rightness of his possession and moved against him.

She knew the moment when he lost control, heard the groan torn from his throat, felt the hard possession of his body. Her passion met his, welcoming it, feeling his harsh need inside her as a joyful victory, fullness, loving. Right. She moved against him again, fire against fire. Then the rhythm was his, theirs, and joy became tangled with impatience, with need, with heat until everything exploded and there was only sensation and loving in the world.

CHAPTER EIGHT

MOLLY woke with the sun on her face and Patrick's arm across her waist, his face nestled against her shoulder. She closed her eyes and let the feel of him soak in.

So it had not been a dream. Her dreams of Patrick were always filled with heat, but the warm security of his arms holding her while he slept was something she had not anticipated in dreams.

Better than fantasy.

When Patrick moved in his sleep, she felt her body respond. When she turned her head, careful not to disturb him, she saw that the sheets were tangled around his limbs. Like Jeremy, she thought with painful tenderness.

She was not going to cry and she was absolutely *not* going to ruin the life of the man she loved by hanging on. Not when she knew she could only bring him a load of scandal.

He did not stir when she slid away, but he came to her later while she was standing under the pounding shower. "There isn't room!" she gasped, but there was.

He took the tiny complimentary shampoo bottle from her hand and lathered the white stuff through her hair. His fingers sent long tingles of heat through her scalp and her body as he massaged the water through her hair, rinsing the soap away. When the water and the hair were streaming down her face and her back, he found a bar of soap from somewhere and drew her back against his hard length while he soaped the rest of her body.

"Oh, Patrick," she whispered. He made her feel so loved, so cherished. She slid her wet arms around his neck, reached up and pulled his lips down to her mouth.

Hours later, tucked into the passenger seat of Patrick's Corvette and driving north again, Molly began to worry.

"Your family are going to think...are going to know——"

"That we're lovers?" His hand found hers and closed over it. There was a faint smile on his lips. "They'll be right, won't they? I told you, Molly, you have to learn not to worry."

"Some things need worrying about." She bit her lip. Like Saul, and tax collectors.

"Hand those things to me." His hand tightened. "I'll look after them for you."

She stared at the highway ahead. Another hour and they would be in Nanaimo. Then Gabriola Island and the cabin. Saul's cabin. The government's cabin.

"I've looked after myself for a long time," she said carefully, because there were no words for what really needed saying. Goodbye. Because Patrick wanted to take over her problems, slay her dragons. Because she must not let the man she loved be hurt by Saul.

"Too long," muttered Patrick. "You've looked after yourself too long."

He stared grimly out the windshield and said flatly, "I want you in my life, Molly. Your problems, whatever the hell they are. Your worries. Your dinosaurs." He shot her one grim look from under lowered brows. "Your love—our love. Our children, Molly, because I've seen you with Jeremy and Sally. You want that, too, as much as I do."

She closed her eyes tightly and whispered, "It can't work." She felt the sick war of dreams and fate tangled in her stomach. What would he think if she threw up?

Right here, all over his beautiful car. She swallowed hard and wished herself anywhere but here at the side of the man she loved. "No," she said painfully. "It won't work. It can't work."

She watched his fingers curl around the steering wheel. "I'll change your mind," he said quietly, and she knew him well enough to know that a quiet-spoken Patrick was at his most determined, that he was a man who got what he wanted in life.

In the end, she would have to run away. Unless she could persuade him that she didn't love him. She hugged herself with arms crossed tightly across her chest. Don't tell lies, and don't run away. Two of her rules, vows made when Carla took in the twelve-year-old Molly and gave her control of her own life. Rules for a girl who had lived in the shadow of a man who didn't believe in rules. She had a collection of them, things she believed in. Be honest with the people you care about. Pay what you owe the day the bill comes.

She shivered in the warm blast of air that came from the heater of Patrick's car, cold because there were no words between them now, only the sick feeling of tension.

They came across on the last ferry of the night, arriving at Gabriola just after eleven. Quiet inside the car, so much unsaid. Molly closed her eyes and tried to feel calm. It was ironic that peaceful Gabriola now had the power to fill her with dread.

Tomorrow was Tuesday. The second working day of the week. Normally, Patrick would have been in his offices in Nanaimo on a Monday, not away in a Victoria luxury hotel with his lover.

What had happened here on the island while they were away in Victoria? Had the bailiffs come? Would Molly find a lock or a seal or whatever they used on the door of her cabin? Would the neighbors know already? Who came to do it anyway? Was it a sheriff's car? Some kind

of Revenue Canada vehicle? The RCMP? There was a
small detachment on Gabriola, just one police car.

When Patrick drove past the farm, the buildings were
dark except for the yard lights that shone on the farmhouse and the barns. "Edward's lights are out too," he
said a moment later. "Presumably they're all sleeping."
He passed his own drive, then turned up hers. The car
bumped slowly over the roughness of the drive and came
to rest in front of her cabin. Patrick put the brake on
and turned to face Molly. His fingers traced the shape
of her cheek.

"I want to be with you tonight." He saw her swallow
and said harshly, "I want all your nights, Molly." She
shook her head, denying her own dream, but he went
on grimly. "When I can't see you, I need to know you're
just a phone call away, that when I come home, it's our
home and if you're not there, you will be soon—because
it's the place we both belong."

She hadn't realized that she was shaking her head again
and again until he stilled the motion with his hands in
her hair. "You love me. I know you do."

"It's impossible."

"Nothing is impossible."

Oh, God! She felt the tears coming, squeezed her lids
tight to try to hold them back. Desperately, she whispered, "I need time. I—I have to...think." To run. Run
away from love.

"How long?"

"I don't know." How long would it take for the due
process of law to break her bubble? "I have to finish
the illustrations for the book. I—I can't concentrate on
it. I—Patrick, I'd make a rotten politician's wife." She
might have managed it, she thought, if it weren't for
Saul.

He jerked impatiently. "Oh, for—I don't believe this
is about politics."

She shook her head, the closest to a lie she had ever come with Patrick. It wasn't about politics. It was about her father.

"I'm in love with you, Molly."

She shuddered. "I can't let you be."

"You're not stupid enough to think you can stop me. Or yourself, for that matter. I'll give you time, Molly, if that's what you need, but you're not getting rid of me." He smiled, and she wondered what it would take to make him give up.

"How long, Molly?"

"How—what?"

"How long? How much... breathing space do you need? How much time to finish the dinosaurs?"

"A week?" She gulped. "Two?" He made an impatient movement and she jerked out, "Ten days."

"Am I supposed to stay away that long? I won't do it, Molly. I need to see you, to know you're all right."

He had taught her joy and love, and she was never going to be all right again. She was greedy, selfish, and she whispered, "I don't want you to stay away." Just a few days. Just until the end. "I need... some distance... and... no talk about the future."

"You'll be mine, Molly." His voice seemed to take hold of her body, her soul. "Talk or no talk, you gave yourself to me the first time you looked into my eyes. Sooner or later, you'll realize it's inevitable."

She fumbled for the handle of the door.

"Good night, my love." That quiet voice was filled with confidence. He knew he owned her heart.

He moved his car slightly as she went up the stairs, shining his lights on the door for her. She felt her heart beat again when she saw that there was nothing unusual on the door. No seal. No padlock. She used the key to unlock it and went inside.

Trouble followed her inside, rubbing against her ankles. Molly found a note on the kitchen counter.

> We fed Trouble and gave her water. She's eating real cat food now. We got some from unkel David and she ate it all up. There's more in the cupboard under the fridge. Hope you had a good holiday. Jeremy

"I'm sorry I forgot you," she whispered, bending down to stroke the sleek fur. How on earth had Jeremy got inside the cabin? She must remember to ask tomorrow. Meanwhile, Trouble was moving urgently back and forth in front of Molly, rubbing, mewing.

The box of cat food was exactly where Jeremy had promised. "I didn't mean to forget you," she told Trouble. "You see, I'm in love. I've never been in love before, and it's turned my brain to mush, I think."

Trouble purred her understanding and attacked the dish of cat food as if she had not eaten for a week. Thank goodness Jeremy had remembered about Trouble. Or was it Patrick who had thought of it? Probably, she decided. He might have asked Jeremy to look after the cat while she was gone. She supposed she was the one who had left the back door unlocked, finally picking up the relaxed attitude of the Gabriolans about locking doors and cars.

She locked up now, because she needed to keep her city habits. She would not be here much longer, not unless someone came up with a miracle. She changed into a nightshirt upstairs, but didn't get into bed. She knew he would call, and when the telephone rang she hurried downstairs to answer it.

"All settled?" he asked. If he had not called, Molly knew she would have lain upstairs, awake and waiting.

"Did you ask Jeremy to look after Trouble?"

"I asked Edward. He's more dependable." There was music behind Patrick's voice. "Edward must have delegated the job. Trouble's there?"

"Yes." In her mind she labeled it as Patrick's music, because she had heard it in the background before when he called her.

"You've tamed that cat, haven't you? Molly's magic. Does she sleep with you?"

"Not so far, but I've been working on it."

"Try *me*," he suggested. "I'll accept. Is it against the rules for me to tell you that I love you?" It was, but she suspected that he did not believe in rules he hadn't made himself. She was smiling when she put the phone down. Maybe, somehow . . . with luck . . .

In the days that followed, Patrick did not stay away, but neither did he talk about tomorrows. Sometimes Molly caught herself wondering if she had imagined those two days in Victoria, fantasized Patrick's intense need of her. There was no sign of it now; he treated Molly with the same casual warmth he showed toward his sister.

While she might have resisted Patrick's continued pursuit of her—just—this new tactic threw her off balance. In Molly's dreams was a new yearning. Her sleep was taken over by something more than fantasy— a deep ache for the man she belonged to. The man who had been determined to have her, until now.

Molly turned around one day at the Hollisons' and caught Patrick's eyes on her. The world faded. Molly could not hear Sally, who was pulling her sweater and asking about Bronty's love life; or Jeremy, who was complaining loudly about having to clear the table. The only reality was Patrick, his eyes holding hers so that she could feel her chest expand when he breathed.

Then it was gone. She saw it happen. Patrick blinked slowly and deliberately replaced the intensity with something that was almost laughter. Waiting. Then she understood. Nothing had changed. Patrick was using deliberate tactics on her. Manipulating her. He was a man who knew how to use the weapons he had to get what he wanted, and he wanted Molly Natham.

Molly, with disaster hovering, and Saul probably somewhere in Europe tossing back a glass of wine and talking about painting.

Sarah Hollison came home, complete with twin babies Tammy and Terry. She invited Molly and Patrick to dinner, presented Molly with a bouquet of yellow roses.

"Molly, thank you." Sarah smiled and the smile was warm, as if Molly really were family, then she added, "Don't forget who your friends are when you need someone."

Edward cooked dinner the day Sarah returned home, gourmet fare that put Molly's plain cooking to shame. Patrick's eyes laughed with her across the table when she saw the gorgeous pineapple-garnished ham that came to the table.

"I told you," he murmured.

"Told her what?" demanded Edward, his worried eyes going over the table, looking for a problem he hadn't seen.

"That you could cook well enough to keep yourself from starving."

Sarah dropped her fork. "You *didn't* make Molly cook your meals?"

"Well," he said hesitantly. "You know I've had to do all that business with the bank, and that hassle with the health inspector and you in hospital."

"Edward! You absolute rat! How could you?"

Molly had to laugh at Edward's look of embarrassment. He shrugged and Molly caught mischief in his eyes. "Actually, it was a nice change. You never do any cooking around here."

The argument that followed moved from heat to laughter. Then after dinner Sarah went up to feed the babies while Edward dragged Patrick off to do the dishes, muttering, "Women don't know their place any more," but Molly wasn't fooled this time.

"You're a menace," she told him. "I'm going in to watch the news."

She curled up on the living-room couch, enjoying the sound of the men's voices from the kitchen, the warmth of the fire crackling in the fireplace, while the announcer on the television set cheerfully reported disasters on the other side of the world.

"So what's new?" asked Patrick as he came in, still rolling his sleeves down.

She smiled. "You had your hands in dishwater?"

"Hmm. Not everything would fit in the machine. Is that who I think it is on the big screen?"

"Who else?" asked Edward, coming in behind Patrick. "Dustin Overley is the political fool of the year."

Patrick watched, his face impassive, one hand in the pocket of his pants. Just another political scandal, but it sounded like the end of Dustin Overley's political career. Molly shivered, staring up at Patrick's intent face.

The camera shifted to a demonstration against an increase in university tuition fees and Edward wondered, "Can he carry it off, do you think?"

Patrick shrugged. "Probably not, it's too late now. He should have come out with it in the first place, or stayed out of politics. Even the courts aren't very sympathetic when it's a politician getting the brunt of the hot Press."

Edward turned his half-worried frown on Molly. "Who the hell would get into politics, eh Molly? Pat's crazy to think of it. Next year on TV we'll be hearing all about that cow Pat killed when he was eighteen."

Patrick laughed. "He's slandering me, Molly. I didn't kill that damned cow."

Edward shrugged, hiding laughter with a frown. "Close enough for the scandal sheets. David told me the cow bloody near died, and all because his kid brother mucked up the feed mix. What do you think, Molly? Unbecoming behavior for an MLA? Right?"

She must have managed to smile, because even Patrick didn't notice anything wrong. Then Sarah came back and worried with Molly about whether she should get a diaper service instead of using disposables, which she knew were a problem to the environment.

"I could wash diapers myself for now, but come the tourist season there won't be time. And there's no diaper service on Gabriola. I can't truck dirty diapers to Nanaimo every day, can I?"

"Patrick could take them in the Corvette," suggested Edward evilly, and they all descended into laughter when Patrick offered to pay for a maid to wash diapers for Sarah. Molly laughed with them, but inside she could feel that sick dread of the future welling up. Sarah might smile at her now, including her as if she were family, but that would change when Saul's disaster struck.

She knew she should keep some emotional distance from Patrick and his family, that it would only be worse later if she let them become part of her. She honestly tried, but Patrick was a casual steamroller who would not take no for an answer, and he made sure that Molly spent most of her evenings with him. Some evenings at the Hollisons', others at the farm. Once in Nanaimo seeing a new *Star Trek* movie with Jeremy and Sally.

He never asked Molly to his house, didn't once come inside her cabin. She had asked for time, and in his way he was giving it to her. He made sure that there were always other people around, but Patrick was always one of them. Waiting.

Ten days, he had said. Ten days for her to finish the illustrations.

Molly was making steady progress on the small paintings that would illustrate Alex's new book. She was also building up one hell of a telephone bill, trying every number in Saul's book. She was not aware of making a conscious decision to stay and ride out the problems to come. But the decision had been made. She wasn't going to run away. If she made it through the ten days without getting locked out of the cabin by the bailiffs, she would somehow find the courage to tell Patrick about the cabin and her father and the tax man.

He wouldn't turn away from her. Not because of Saul, anyway, although she was beginning to believe that he would be furiously angry when he realized just how big a problem Molly had been hiding from him. He had grown up in a family that believed in turning to the people you loved for help and support. He would think that if she loved him she should trust him with this.

Trust him with a problem that could spell doom to any chances he had of winning a seat in the legislature? She turned it around in her mind. What if Patrick led her into a situation that made it impossible for her to sell her paintings? She couldn't think of how that could happen, but was positive he would never do that to her. How could she ruin his future? Yet how could she leave him, knowing that he loved her?

Her time with Patrick had a quality that made disaster seem part of another universe. Molly found that she could smile and laugh, that sometimes Saul and Revenue Canada seemed like a dream. The dinosaurs took color and life under her brush. She worked every morning from dawn until noon; then she put her brushes down and waited for the telephone to ring, because Patrick called every day just after noon.

Inconsequential talk, yet each morning she worked with the warm anticipation of those few moments to come. Patrick told her about computer glitches and minor staff problems, and asked how the dinosaurs were behaving. Molly told him about the deer who wandered into her clearing, about Trouble, who had taken to sleeping curled up in the corner while she painted.

Unimportant conversation, yet she felt cherished without his ever saying a word about loving. After he hung up, she would make herself a sandwich and take it outside, walking through the trees and letting her mind fill with the next layer of ideas for the illustrations. The pictures were painting themselves, flowing as if they had already been created in full detail and color, in her mind.

She finished the illustrations nine days into Patrick's hands-off campaign, in mid-morning.

Done! Molly poured herself a cup of coffee in the kitchen, then came back and stared at the last illustration. She knew this book would be the best she had ever done. Bronty and Terry and Rex were somehow more alive than ever before.

Done, finished, and, if she was not running, tonight it would be time to tell Patrick about the strings attached to Saul's cabin.

She pushed that necessity away and worked slowly on packing the pictures for shipping. She used acrylic paints, quick drying, so it was safe to pack them together with layers of tissue between. She arranged them in order and slipped them into a sturdy cardboard envelope with Alex's manuscript. She could feel her heart thudding as she sealed the envelope.

Tuesday. Almost noon. She wrote her agent's address on the envelope, then got out her "fragile" stickers and "do not bend" notices and plastered them on front and back.

It was right that the telephone should ring just as she was lying the package down on the counter. Patrick.

"Hi!" She was breathless, her eyes on the package still, her mind on how she could string the words together.

"You've been chasing me around like a damned bloodhound! What the devil do you think you're doing?"

Saul! She sank down on the sofa and whispered, "Listen, you've got to come back here, right now. I—you've got to talk to the tax people and——"

"Molly, are you nuts? Do you know what you're suggesting, girl?"

She closed her lips and bit back the desperate plea—promise me! Saul's promises were worthless; he would say whatever he was forced to, then do what he wanted. "Where are you?"

"Overseas. It's the middle of the bloody night, too, and I've been getting calls from half the people I know. Did you call *everybody*?"

"Everyone I could think of, and they all said they hadn't a clue where you were." She sighed. "Saul, how long do you think you'll stay free, when the government comes after you and every weirdo and artist on the Continent knows your whereabouts?"

"Don't lecture me, Molly." He sounded like a small boy, complaining, "I stopped hanging around for criticism when I quit school."

"Saul, listen to me. I—you've got to come back and straighten this thing out. There's a final notice in the mail from Revenue Canada, and if you don't do something——"

"I'm not paying it."

"Saul——"

"No, damn it! Listen, girl! I didn't ask for Medicare. I didn't ask for roads or schools or idiots in Ottawa

spending my money on new buildings and secretaries!
Income tax! Do you know how it started, Molly?"

"Yes," she said wearily. She had heard this before.

"Do you know what they called it? The Income War
Tax Act! 1917! And it was temporary, Molly! Just to
support the war effort. Temporary, except that it's
forever, and I bloody didn't ask for it and I won't pay
it!"

"Saul listen to me! It's a criminal offense. Tax evasion.
Don't you under——? Don't you dare hang up on me!
You—oh, damn!"

He was gone and it was no use dreaming, thinking
there was some tidy way to clean up his problems. Some
way to keep Patrick in her life without ruining him. This
wasn't a landlord she could talk to, a grocery store owner
who had stopped extending credit. This was the government, and criminal charges because even when they
foreclosed on the cabin it wouldn't come to two hundred
thousand dollars and Saul would be a fugitive. She put
the receiver down slowly, wondering why her eyes felt
so dry and everything so odd and frozen. She would
have to go away, run because Saul had fled one more
responsibility.

Incredibly, the telephone rang again. She jerked the
receiver up to her ear. If she could find the right words,
somehow make him realize how important this was.

"Thank God you called back! Saul, please listen to
me. You've got to come back, straighten out this mess!
It's so important! Please! Oh, God, Saul! Don't do this
to me! I..."

Silence.

"Saul——?"

"It's Patrick, Molly."

She closed her eyes.

"Molly, are you all right?"

"Yes—no. I——"

"I'll be right there."

"No! No, Patrick! I——"

But it was her day for listening to the dead sound of the dial tone. He was coming, and this time he would make her tell him all the details, the whole mess. Patrick, and he would take over. For Molly. But what could he do? The government wanted money. Taxes due, and one could hardly blame them. Molly's ill-gotten cabin wasn't going to satisfy the debt, wouldn't be enough by a long way. Saul's new paintings might have covered it, but he'd stolen them away.

Smuggling, Babette had said.

Oh, God! What if Patrick decided to pay the debt himself? Molly had no idea whether he had that kind of money, but she had a sick conviction that he could probably raise it. A debt, paying forever because he loved Molly Natham.

She couldn't let him get tangled in her mess, Saul's mess. She squeezed her eyes tight and admitted that she could not stop him. He would come, and...

Soon. Right away, he had said. Of course, he had to wait for the next ferry. But when he came—when he came, she had better be gone. Molly dashed out to the van, threw open the door and realized she had no keys. Oh, God! She had left the van door unlocked, must have caught Patrick's casual attitude to locks. As if she were a Gabriolan, and belonged here.

She hurried back to the cabin, grabbed her purse and her keys. Must get out of here, before he came. Must——

Trouble was standing in the middle of the kitchen, mewing. Molly's fingers clenched on the keys. "I have to, Trouble. He'll look after you. I have to go. You've got to understand."

The cat glared at her, tail stiffening.

"Come with me, then," Molly said tentatively. Trouble hissed and jumped back.

What time had Patrick called? Before one. He would catch the one-thirty, drive off on his side at ten to two. Or would he be able to make the twelve-thirty ferry? Molly glanced at the clock wildly, wondered where she was going to hide herself and her van to avoid driving past Patrick as he came home.

"Listen, Trouble, I'm going. Do you want to come or not?"

Patrick always took North Road. So if she drove to the ferry on South Road, he would not see her leaving. If she got under way soon enough, she could drive all the way to the ferry terminal and park on that side road while the *Quinsam* docked. Then, when she saw the Corvette drive off the ferry, she could drive on, leaving on the same ferry that brought him.

Yes. That was the only way. Otherwise, when he got to her cabin and found the van gone, he would turn right around and head for the ferry. He would know she had run, would stop her.

"Trouble, come here. Come on, kitty. Come to Molly." The cat hissed and backed away. When the cat turned and ran out of the door, Molly felt sick to her stomach. Maybe she had some kind of stomach trouble growing on her, because this kept happening. Pain and nausea and bleak grayness.

"Trouble! Come on, honey! Come here, kitty." Molly brushed at her cheeks. Damn, she wasn't going to cry over abandoning a cat, was she? Not when the world was coming to pieces.

"Trouble! Here, kitty, kitty!"

Maybe Trouble had the right idea. What kind of a home could Molly give a black-and-white cat? The long drive back east. She *supposed* she was going back to

Ottawa. Trouble would hate the trip, would probably hate living in the middle of tall buildings and traffic.

Molly went back to the cabin, stared at the padded envelope lying on the counter. She had forgotten all about that. Her bread and butter, and she had better start remembering. From now on, there would be no Patrick in her life, looking after the details. Caring.

She walked slowly up the stairs, the package of illustrations held tightly in her left hand. Pack. She had to pack. Her acrylic paints. Her tape collection. She tumbled the paints into their box and got it fastened, brushing tears away angrily. Damn Saul! It was one thing being impulsive and temperamental, but he had actively messed up her life this time.

"One of these days he's got to learn to pay the piper," she muttered. "Does he think the damned piper will just go away?"

She had forgotten her brushes. And the pastels. Her sketch block. Damn! She opened the wooden paint box and stuffed in the pastels and the brushes, knocked over a small container of charcoals. Oh, hell! She started to bend down, picking them up, then abandoned the impulse. No time, and if Saul could leave the place a mess then so could Molly!

She took the paint box and her sketch block, added the envelope that she had almost forgotten once again. Outside, she tried again, calling, "Trouble? Trouble! Here, kitty!"

It was no use. What time was it? She dashed back to the house and it was twenty to two. The ferry would be docking in ten minutes, He must not have made the twelve-thirty, or he would be here by now.

How could she have taken so long? Ten minutes, and he would be on the island, determined to solve her problems even if it destroyed him.

Nobody solved Saul's problems. If anybody knew that, Molly did. She blinked and managed to focus on the driveway. She had to leave the cat, but she would call Patrick from somewhere along the road. *Please look after my cat.*

That was what Saul had done. Run, and left Molly with the pieces. Molly had no choice but to run too, but she would not call. Patrick and Jeremy would look after Trouble without her asking.

Sarah was on the road, waving at Molly's van as she turned out of the driveway. Sarah, who had been doubtful at first and was a friend now, standing there with a handful of mail and a smile on her lips, expecting Molly to stop and say hello.

Molly didn't stop, but she did try to return the smile. Somehow, though, she could not make her lips curve and she saw Sarah in the rearview mirror after she had passed, staring after the van in confusion.

Molly turned left off McNaughton road, then realized her mistake. She had turned the wrong way, toward North Road. She had to go on South Road, to avoid Patrick. All right. Calm down. She would stop at the farm, pull into the driveway and turn around, get going the other way. Oh, God! She had to get off this island, somehow make it from here and now to the end of this nightmare day!

She stopped with a jerk beside the farm. Better hurry. Patrick would come soon. What time was it? What had happened to her watch? It had gone missing at least a week ago and Molly had not bothered to look for it. Time simply had not seemed important.

What was she, some crazy dreamer to think she could wander around and ignore things like time and realities?

She started into the driveway of the farm, then slammed on the brakes when she saw David's truck coming out. "Coming to visit?" he shouted from his open window.

"Just turning around. Sorry!" Was that her voice?

"Go ahead! I'm in no hurry." His stern face was smiling, because Molly was almost one of the family. Patrick had told Molly he loved her, wanted her as his wife. Had he told David, too? And Sarah? Perhaps he had not needed to. The love was in his eyes and his voice. No hurry, David had said, but there was. Molly stalled the van, got it started again and finally got back out on the road, turned toward South Road this time. She saw a cloud of dust behind and wondered sickly if that was Patrick.

Too soon. Let it be too soon. Molly was beyond being sensible. It was all a jumble. Saul and the cabin and Patrick who would look after her no matter what the cost. He loved her, and she must not let him, must get away before he came and she couldn't stop him and could not bear to hurt him.

"No," she whispered, but there was no one to hear, and that was on a par with her effectiveness in saying no these days.

She jolted on to South Road and found herself behind one of those trucks that worked trimming tree branches away from the power lines. The thing didn't seem to be in operation, but it was crawling along South Road. What time was it? If she got to the terminal at the wrong time, she would meet the Corvette coming the other way. What would Patrick do if that happened? Stop? Turn around and come after her?

Should she drive off on one of the side roads, park somewhere in the middle of the trees on an old logging road? Hide?

She was later than she had thought. The ferry was in, a stream of cars coming at her from the opposite direction. She didn't see the white sports car, but when she drove into the lane for ferry traffic the ramp was just going up. She watched the *Quinsam* leaving, without her.

Patrick was here on the island, and she had an hour to wait for the next ferry. No, the next one didn't leave until quarter past three, a fifteen-minute hiccup in the schedule that Molly hadn't managed to figure out yet. She would have to ask Patrick about it some time.

Patrick. He would be at the cabin by now. He might go to Sarah's next, or to the farm. Sarah and David would tell him Molly had gone off in a mad state, driving wildly and not knowing how to smile. He would be worried, would think she had run off on some emergency, would come after her. She sat, frozen, her hands clenched on the wheel. It seemed like forever, but she jumped when the door jerked open beside her. Patrick grabbed her arm with hard fingers, but it was the anger in his voice that made her wince.

"What the hell do you imagine you're going to solve by running away?" He leaned part way into the car, gripped the steering wheel above her hand and demanded. "Look at me, damn it! Molly!"

"I'm just——"

"Your things are strewn all over the cabin. Paints gone, and the dinosaurs. Why the hell would you have to run like that? Damn it! Why?"

She gulped. She had once thought an angry Patrick would be easier to handle than the quietly determined man. She had been wrong.

"Molly?" Harsh. Demanding. "You were desperate on the phone. You thought I was Saul. What's he done to you, Molly? To make you run and——"

"I wanted to get away from you."

"You—why?"

She swallowed the lump that rose at the lie. "I don't... love you. I don't want..." Oh, God! She was not going to cry, was she? Not now! Later, but not now. She blinked, hard, and felt the hot tears subside only slightly.

"You're lying."

She stared at his hand on the steering wheel. "Yes," she admitted. "I'm lying." She saw his hand jerk, clenched her own fingers around the steering wheel. "I had to get away."

"Molly, tell me——"

She interrupted him with a wild laugh. "Oh, God, Patrick! Don't tell me you're going to look after it! Whatever it is, you'll solve it for me!"

He took her chin roughly with his hand, forced her to meet his eyes. "I'll look after it, Molly. Whatever it is."

"I don't want you to!" She gritted her eyes closed, said harshly, "Let me go! That's what I want! I want you to take your hands off me and let me go in peace. I don't want looking after and caring for and...and... or..."

His fingers dug in. "You're running away from *me*?"

In a terrible way, it was true. She blinked her eyes hard and stared back at him. Please, don't let the tears come yet! "Yes. From—from you. It—I—you smother me! For God's sake, Patrick! Let go of me! Let me go! Please!"

He released her so abruptly that she could still feel the place where his fingers had dug into the flesh under her jaw. She had never seen that look in his eyes before. She whispered, "Please, Patrick, will you look after Trouble? She wouldn't come with me."

Something like a shudder went through his body, then he turned and walked away. She watched him all the way back to his car. He had parked four cars back in the ferry lineup, but all that way, he did not look back at her once. There was a woman in a Mazda just behind

Molly's van, staring curiously. Molly didn't notice, but eventually she did realize that the door to her van was still open.

That told her more than anything else that she had succeeded in convincing Patrick McNaughton she wasn't his business. Even an angry Patrick would have closed the door before he walked away from her, not left it open to get sideswiped by a car coming down the traffic lane alongside.

She heard the slam of Patrick's door farther back in the lineup, then the engine roar that changed to a powerful whine as the tires screamed. When the howl of the Corvette's engine died away in the distance, Molly's tears finally came.

CHAPTER NINE

MOLLY could not remember driving through most of British Columbia. She remembered the ferry lineup leaving Vancouver Island, scrambling for her purse and wondering if she had left it behind, not caring much . . . wondering how she had paid for the ferry off Gabriola and remembering that it was free. One paid only when going out to the island.

Pay to get on, get off free. Ironic, because that was backward. She had gone to Gabriola for free, riding on Saul's deceptive gift. But leaving was going to cost her. The painful shadows of loving would be with her always.

She slept in a motel somewhere along the freeway, stumbled out to the van the next morning and started driving again. British Columbia was a fog of mechanical driving. Alberta was clearer. By the time she crossed the border into the province of Saskatchewan, she was able to wonder where she was going.

She stopped in the city of Saskatoon, realizing that she could not drive blindly forever. For one thing, she would drive straight off the freeway on one of those slow curves. She told herself that stopping was a good sign. If she could think this clearly with only four days' driving behind her, she might somehow manage to live the next few decades without Patrick.

Was Patrick looking after Trouble?

The next day, Molly telephoned her old roommate in Ottawa and asked if her bedroom was taken yet. "Sorry," said Wendy. "It went the day after you left. There's the couch if you need it, though."

"Thanks, but I need a studio." That was a lie, because Molly might never be able to paint again, but it was impossible to accept Wendy's invitation. Impossible to be a guest on someone else's couch with the tears still coming without warning. She needed a door she could close. "Do you know of anything, Wendy?"

"Hmm... Well, there's this two-bedroom I heard about, but it's kind of oppressive. Furnished, though."

Better to know where she was going. Maybe another five hundred miles along the way and she would be ready to call Carla, but her aunt would ask questions that Molly was not ready to answer. She thought fleetingly of Saul, a vague worry as she was driving around the northern shore of Lake Superior, anything to forget that look in Patrick's eyes when she screamed at him to get away from her, to let her go.

She was *not* going to start crying again. Concentrate on the details, anything but the memories and the broken dreams. Like how much money did she have to pay all these darned credit-card slips for gas when the bills came in? That was the important thing. With fuel at fifty or more cents a liter, she had better think about money.

Concentrate on numbers, not on Patrick tearing away from the ferry in the Corvette. Patrick, who was always so controlled, except in her arms where the calm exterior dissolved and turned to flames.

Three thousand miles, more or less, from Ottawa to the ferry at Vancouver. Then back again. What kind of mileage did she get on the highway in this van? Three thousand miles twice. That would be about ten thousand kilometers, and it was time she stopped doing everything in miles per gallon. Liters per kilometre. No, that was wrong. Miles—no, kilometers per liter. Oh, damn! What did it matter. Who cared?

*   *   *

Ottawa was blooming, flowers lifting their petals to the spring sunshine, the parliament buildings standing on the hill with their green cooper roofs turned to the sky. Time had stood still. A month was nothing. Canada's capital city was unchanging.

As Wendy had promised, the new apartment was depressing, nothing-colored walls and indifferent but clean furniture. Molly transferred the contents of her van to drawers and cupboards. She pushed the bed in the second bedroom to the wall and set up her sketching easel. No music. Her tapes and her stereo were back on Gabriola Island, in the cabin.

Had anyone slapped an official lock on the door of Saul's cabin yet? Saul's cabin. Her cabin. The government's. She supposed she should contact the lawyer who had done the transfer, but hadn't the energy to do anything but wonder how Saul had tricked her into his problems after fourteen years of keeping clear. By the age of twelve, Molly had learned far too much about looking after her irresponsible parent. At twenty-six, surely she knew better than to feel responsible? Different if she could actually do something, but he had hung up on her, and he would hang up again if she ran him to earth.

This new thing, the urge to find him and shake him and tell him he'd ruined her life... No, there was no sense in that either.

She finally called Carla and got thoroughly bawled out. "Molly, where the hell are you? I've been calling and calling that number out west—there's never an answer."

"Sorry. I'm back in Ottawa, tied up with painting a new picture." Lies. How had she come to telling lies to people she loved?

"That's why I've been calling you, among other things. Your agent's wild to get hold of you. Something about all those full-size paintings selling, and when could you do a showing because the gallery wants to set up something for the spring?''

A year ago, when Molly had realized that the children's books were selling quite well, she had started doing full-size dinosaur paintings. Her agent had been skeptical that gallery paintings of children's fantasies would sell, but he had agreed to try. ''I'll call him,'' she promised Carla. ''Getting ready for a showing will keep me busy, anyway.''

''I thought you said you *were* busy? Painting a new something, you said. Molly, just *why* are you back? I assumed you'd got bushed out there in the wilds, but——''

''It's not exactly the back of the beyond,'' Molly said, automatically defending Gabriola. ''It's beautiful,'' she added, because Aunt Carla believed that the civilized world ended at the western boundary of metro Toronto.

''If it's so great out there, why didn't you stay?''

She put a shrug into her voice. ''As you said, the cabin had strings attached. Can——?''

''What strings?''

Molly grimaced. She should have known she would end up saying too much. ''It's complicated, Aunt Carla. Too involved for the telephone. Can you send me those cases I stored with you? I need the clothes.''

After she said goodbye to Aunt Carla, Molly called her agent and let him bully her into agreeing to do twenty paintings for next February. She bought canvases and replenished her acrylics and brushes, but the light in the spare bedroom was terrible and nothing she painted looked right. Perhaps it was the light in her imagination that had dimmed. She knew she had to get back to the old Molly somehow, back to caring about today and tomorrow and the rest of her life.

She went for long walks along the Rideau Canal, but whenever she returned to her dingy makeshift studio the dinosaur on her canvas stubbornly refused to come to life. Should she try painting something else? Trees or flowers? Patrick's face, his dark brows lowered over those black eyes as he read her soul? Yes, one day she would paint him. When she was ready.

Did Patrick ever dream of her? She thought not, because she had seen his face and knew she had killed his love with words. One day she would see his name in the news, she supposed. The new MLA in the British Columbia legislature. Then, after he had conquered that arena, he might turn up in federal politics here at Ottawa. Years from now, Molly might walk past parliament hill and see a black limousine drive up with Patrick in the back seat, a beautiful stranger at his side.

Of course he would marry, have children. Without Molly. She turned away from the lazy flow in the Rideau Canal and hurried back to her apartment. She had to stop these thoughts, had to find something to erase Patrick's image from her mind. At least let it fade, she thought desperately.

She opened the security door and went to the elevator, admitting bleakly that she did not want Patrick to fade, that she would hold him in her heart forever. If she could go back and beg him to love her again, she would, but nothing had changed. Molly Natham was still a time-bomb for any man destined for a life in the public eye.

The elevator wasn't coming. Molly pushed the button again, but the indicator seemed stuck on the seventh floor. She shrugged and went to the fire stairs. One of these days she would get angry about something. She would be on her way back to life the day she found she could care about something other than the man who had loved her and the cat she had abandoned.

Four flights of stairs, then she pushed open the heavy fire door and emerged in her own corridor. At first, she did not see the man standing near her apartment door. Then she did, and she stopped in mid-stride, frozen. Patrick, leaning against the wall. Waiting.

It had to be another trick of her mind. Patrick. Here. He turned and she knew it was real. His eyes. In her fantasies, it was always love in his eyes.

Anger, she thought. Freezing fury, hot ice. If he were driving, he would be jamming the gears with a hard rage, not spinning the tires. How had he got into the building? This was supposed to be a security building, but she supposed that would not stop Patrick. Why had he come? Patrick, glaring at her with derision or hatred in his eyes, not love.

Her fingers were clenched, nails digging into her palms. Somehow, the pain got through and she unclenched them and took one step after another until she ended up beside her own door. "What—why are you here?"

He jerked his head toward her apartment door. "Open it."

She fumbled in her bag, but the keys evaded her. He took the bag from her, demanding, "Which key?"

"The . . . ah—that one."

Why was he here? Not smiling, but grim and threatening. She followed him into her own apartment and he stood a few feet inside, looking around slowly, taking everything in. She tried to see it through his eyes and it looked about the same as always. Bare. Empty. Lonely. Why had he come? His eyes finished their circuit and came to rest on her face.

"So this is your preference, Molly?"

"It's what I could find on short notice." Her hands tangled together. "Why are you here, Patrick?"

He laughed harshly. "What's the matter, Molly? Are you afraid I want *you*?"

She winced. "Did you come here to hurt me?" He had a right, she supposed, but she had not known that he could hate with the same passion that had fueled his loving.

He paced across the empty living room and glared at the uncomfortable couch, demanding, "Where do you work? Here?"

"The door on the right."

She followed him, standing in the doorway watching as he studied the dinosaur on her studio easel. He did not need to be an artist to know it was no good.

"Bloody-minded dinosaur," Molly said uncomfortably. "I don't think he wants to be immortalized on canvas." Patrick did not laugh. He might never laugh for her again. "Patrick, how did you find me? I didn't— didn't expect you to try."

"No?" He turned to look at her and she could see the lines of weariness around his eyes. "You made it perfectly clear you didn't want following."

"How?" It didn't matter, except that she could not imagine how he could have found her. "Carla? But you don't know her surname, do you? And in Toronto— well, there have to be pages of Wilsons." He shrugged and she guessed, "Saul's address book? Back in the cabin?"

He laughed, but it was only a sound, did not climb as far as his eyes, or cut into the laughter lines at the sides of his mouth. "If you left any clues back in the cabin, they weren't much use. The whole place is sealed up under court order. You knew that?"

She nodded mutely and his mouth hardened. He said, "I came for your power of attorney."

"What?" Confused, she squeaked, "My—why?"

He lifted his shoulders, dropped them again and glared at the poor dinosaur who stood so stiffly on the canvas. "You'll find out soon enough, won't you?"

She was frightened, knew this was way beyond her control. "That's...ridiculous! What do you want with—why should I give you my—why?"

"Why? Perhaps because you trust me." He made it sound a black joke. She spread her hands helplessly, but there was no softening in his eyes.

"What are you intending to do, Patrick?"

"I'm going to get back what's yours."

"You——"

"Yes," he said grimly. "I'm going after your bloody father. Make him pay his own debts."

"You—you're crazy," she spluttered. "He won't. He would never—you can't make him."

"You're wrong." He was growing impatient. Patrick, who was always willing to wait if it was worth it. Where was the lover she had known? What had she done to the tenderness in his eyes? And why had she done it, if he was still going to get mixed up in this mess?

He pushed past her. She followed him through the corridor and into her bedroom where he jerked open the cupboard door, stared into the darkness for a moment, then pulled out a suitcase.

"Patrick, what are you doing?"

"Start packing."

She licked her lips uneasily. "Patrick, if you knew Saul, you'd know there's no way anybody can make him face up to his responsibilities."

He pulled a handful of hangers out of the cupboard, blouses trailing as he dropped them on the bed. "Did you bring all this from the cottage?"

"No, I—I left some things with my aunt when I went west. My things are mostly still back on...on Gabriola."

He went back for the last of the hanging clothes. She shifted uncomfortably, aware that there was no warmth in his eyes. No feeling in his voice, either, as he said, "You left in quite a hurry, didn't you?"

"Does it matter now?" Thank God the tears had all dried up. She had cried for a week, then her eyes had gone hot and dry and even now she felt nothing much, even with Patrick standing only a hand's reach away. Just that familiar feeling of nausea that she hadn't felt since she left Gabriola. Not ulcers, just love gone sour.

He was throwing underwear and cosmetics into her suitcase in a jumble. She said dully, "Didn't you hear me? You can't make Saul do anything. You probably can't even find him. I couldn't. If you knew him as I do——"

He swung on her and she jerked back, frightened at the fury in his eyes. "If you knew anything about *me*, Molly, you'd know that you're wrong. Now, get packed. I'm taking you home."

Home? She gulped. "I don't want you to—I——" He reached for her and she screamed, "Let go of me! You can't force me to go with you!"

His laugh was harsh. "Can't I?"

"I don't want——"

"I could care less what you want. Not any more. You're packing, coming with me, or I'll pick you up and carry you out of here, kicking and screaming if you want, but you're coming."

She licked her lips uneasily. The mood he was in, he would not hesitate to toss her over his shoulder and carry her out like a sack of potatoes; and if anyone tried to stop him it would make no difference.

"Forget it, Molly. Don't expect reason from me. I'm so bloody furious, I could throttle you. Now get packed. I'll give you ten minutes."

"Ten minutes? That's ridiculous. I'm not going." Another lie, she realized miserably. Even with his eyes harsh and hating her, she would pack and walk away from places a lot more appealing than this dismal apartment if he asked.

"Ten minutes," he repeated. "And if you're not ready, I'll carry you out of here." He sent a scornful glance around the jumble he'd made of her clothing. "You shouldn't have any trouble. You've got some practice. It couldn't have taken you much longer than that to clear out of the cabin at Gabriola."

He had threatened to toss her over his shoulder and carry her out, and she ached for him to touch her. She would be in his arms then, and the anger would melt, draining away and leaving only love in his eyes.

He left her with the mess in the bedroom, called from the kitchenette a moment later, "Are the dishes yours?"

"No."

Ten minutes, he had said, but it was more like an hour. An hour for Patrick to organize Molly's few possessions into boxes and instruct the caretaker about their disposition. An hour until he carried Molly's suitcase out to a rental car in front of the building.

"Get in," he told her. "I'll bring the rest." The rest consisted of the dinosaur canvas, Molly's wooden paint box and her easel. Everything else was in the hands of the caretaker.

"What about my van?"

"Where is it?"

"Parking lot. Under the building." She couldn't even talk any more. Her words were turning as jerky and harsh as his.

He held out his hand for the keys. She didn't even ask him what he was going to do about the van. This Patrick was frightening, determined not to listen to any protest she made. She wondered why he was bothering with her at all when there was no tenderness or softness in his eyes or his voice.

No love left. Did he hate her? Did a man grimly go into battle for a woman he hated? How was she going to stop him? He said he was going to make Saul pay his debts, but he would only hurt himself with masses of horrible publicity. Saul's carefree innocence was unconquerable.

Speeding along the Queensway with Patrick's face grim and the car moving too fast, Molly worried, "You shouldn't speed here. They patrol the Queensway pretty diligently."

No answer, just a hard muscle jumping at the point of his jaw. She looked away from him. "Where are we going?"

"Ottawa International."

"You mean *airport*?"

He did not answer, but shortly they were driving past a security guard, coming to a stop beside a hangar. There were two sleek, small jets on the tarmac. Patrick got out of the van and handed the rental car keys to a young businessman dressed in a suit and a helpful face. Her van keys, too, she thought, but she couldn't hear the instructions Patrick rapped out as the young man nodded and adjusted his tie nervously.

Young yes-man on the way up, she decided, watching them. Then someone touched her arm and said, "This way, ma'am. It's ready."

"It" was one of the jets. Molly followed the uniformed man inside, sat where she was told and agreed that she would keep her seat belt fastened until they were up.

"Is this a Lear jet?" It was the only kind of corporate jet she knew of, but the pilot shook his head.

"De Haviland," he informed her. "Beautiful machine. You won't even know it when we're in the air. We'll be in Vancouver before you know it."

Vancouver?

Patrick appeared and belted himself into the chair opposite hers. She said nervously, "I thought you might send me off into the sunset alone."

He did not laugh. If she had any sense, she would stop trying to change that grim expression, but she wished that Patrick would smile at her just once. Wished she could go into his arms and have the power to turn the hardness back into love. She stared out the window. Buildings passing by the windows. "Is this your plane?"

"No. It belongs to a company I've got an interest in."

"I suppose you've got *interests* strewn all over the country?" Depressing thought. She closed her eyes and said wearily, "I suppose you're filthy rich. You must be, to go tearing across the continent in style like this."

He sighed. "Don't swear, Molly. It doesn't suit you."

She was *not* going to cry! She had promised herself she would not cry in front of him, and damn it! She wouldn't.

"How *did* you find me?"

"The Molly Alex books. The publisher. Your agent." He made it sound a boring piece of detective work. He must care, mustn't he? Otherwise, why all this? Or was it only stubbornness? She grimaced, because he certainly had plenty of that in his nature. Pig-headed right now, she thought. Blindly stubborn, determined to interfere.

She was never going to stop loving him. It would be with her forever, ready to sneak out and knock her down whenever she thought she'd grown some immunity to the memories.

Memories. Victoria. Lying sheltered in his arms as the horse clopped along the streets. Watching as he cradled little Tammy in his arms. Listening to his voice as they walked through the darkness under the trees on Gabriola.

When Ottawa had turned to a patchwork quilt down below, he looked at her and said tonelessly, ''Get some sleep.''

''How long will it be?''

''Long enough for you to sleep.''

She stared at his impassive face, searching for an elusive something she thought she had seen. As if he *wanted* to make her angry? But why?

The bed was behind a partition. Molly pulled the thick curtain closed and lay down, succumbing to the dizzy luxury of sleep almost at once. Weeks of sleepless nights, and now for the first time she felt secure, safe. The man on the other side of the partition might be angry, pigheaded, and miles from the tender, wild lover of her dreams. But he was Patrick, and if he was in charge of things there really wasn't much need to worry. No, she thought groggily. That was wrong, exactly backward. She must not let . . . must not . . .

She woke in the early afternoon somewhere in the skies of British Columbia. Time had rolled backward, the sun still high in the sky when it should be dark. She got up and tidied herself.

Patrick was reading what looked like a long corporate report. Not numbers. Words, page after page of words. Molly picked up a magazine from a rack and spent the hour until they landed turning pages and pulling her eyes from one word to another.

In Vancouver, Patrick delivered her in silence to the twentieth floor of a building in the financial district. Soft carpets, a string of long names announcing what had to be an outrageously expensive firm of barristers and solicitors. Past normal office hours, but downstairs there had been a security guard to sign them in.

In the twentieth-floor office, Patrick stood at a full-length window, staring out at the skyscrapers while the lawyer took her through a mess of paperwork. Molly listened through to the end, then she stared at the forms, not at the lawyer or at Patrick, and announced grimly, "I'm not taking legal action against my own father. I won't."

The lawyer used his million-dollar voice. "Miss Natham, this claim counters the government's charge against the property. Your property, not your father's. The settlement of the tax liability is a separate issue which these forms do not address."

Molly folded her hands in her lap. "It's the government's property. They've got a right to it. I don't care about the cabin."

The lawyer's eyes met Patrick's over her head. "The issue would simplify if we abandoned claim to the property."

Patrick shook his head. "No. It's hers. It was given to her."

Molly thought that there wasn't a chance the courts would see things Patrick's way. She leaned forward and pointed, "I'm not signing that one."

"Miss Natham, you're mistaken if you feel your father can get away with this. He's far too well-known a figure, with showings all over the western world. His paintings will be seized. Governments work together on these things, you know."

She did know. She couldn't believe that Saul didn't know as well, but it was Patrick she wanted to protect if she could.

The lawyer warned, "Your father is in grave danger of being prosecuted criminally. Tax evasion is no trivial matter." His eyes brushed over to the man standing by the window. "I've been retained to represent both you and your father in this matter. Your cooperation will help everyone involved, your father included.''

She looked at Patrick, the nausea washing over her. He was going to try to bail Saul out. She asked quietly, ''Can I stop you?''

''No.''

She rubbed a harried hand along the worry line that was turning into a permanent part of her forehead, then hugged herself tightly and said miserably, ''I don't want you to get hurt trying to straighten out my life.''

It was the first time in two days that he had looked at her without anger in his eyes. He said quietly, ''You don't have any choice in this, Molly. Just sign the papers.''

CHAPTER TEN

SARAH greeted Molly with a hug, a gesture of affection that was nearly Molly's undoing.

"You look terrible," Sarah said warmly. "Exhausted. Patrick, you get her bags. Edward, we'll put her dinner on a tray. She's too tired to make conversation. Thank goodness Jeremy and Sally are asleep, or they'd be all over her!"

Sarah led Molly to one of the guest rooms upstairs. "I wish we could have you downstairs, but the twins have filled everything up. And up here, there are guests crawling everywhere now. Sorry, but it's May and that's life. Just ignore them, will you, and for goodness' sake don't let that man at the end of the corridor trick you into doing his laundry for him."

Sarah bustled around the guest room, turning the bed back, pulling the chair out from the desk. "You can eat here. Unless you prefer pandemonium downstairs? Tammy and Terry are turning colicky. Not tonight, I think, eh?"

"I'm not really hungry at all." Molly chewed on her lip. "Sarah, you don't need to wait on me. I—Patrick really shouldn't have brought me here. I don't know why he did."

Sarah said warmly, "Where else would he bring you? I know he's in a terrible temper, but you don't need to worry about anything. Pat's very good at looking after problems." Sarah frowned and said decisively, "You've got to eat, Molly, hungry or not. You look terrible. I don't suppose my brother has helped any, ranting and raving all over the continent.''

Patrick came into the bedroom with Molly's suitcase at that moment, and Sarah swung on him. ''You listen to me, Patrick Dougall McNaughton! You're leaving Molly alone until she's had a good rest!''

Personally, Molly thought he was glad to leave her in Sarah's hands. He had what he wanted. The power of attorney, his right to fight for the cabin she would never be able to live in again. There was no love left. Not even hate, just anger.

She did not understand this anger. Was it some self-destructive urge to fight battles that weren't his? That didn't sound much like the Patrick she knew, the quiet fighter who knew what he wanted and kept his strategy behind laughing eyes.

Heaven knew, she could be wrong. She was obviously no judge of other people, at least not of Gabriolans. She would have sworn Sarah would turn wary and suspicious when Saul's troubles rained down on Molly, but instead her hostess was rustling around with trays and concern and protective motherly clucking.

They were all treating Molly like a child. Even Edward's dry humor was a little more careful the next morning, a little more than vaguely worried. And Patrick was nowhere in sight.

Molly kept expecting him to turn up. She persuaded Sarah to let her help make up the guests' beds, but she tensed every time she heard a door opening or closing downstairs.

He came in the evening, demanding quietly, ''Molly, come into the office.'' Edward's office, she supposed, or Sarah's. Molly was uncertain who did the paperwork in this bed and breakfast. The labor was divided between Sarah and Edward in a haphazard fashion that worked like clockwork.

Patrick closed the door to the office, walked to the desk and stared out of the window. "Sit down, Molly. I want contacts. Places. The people your father knows in the art world. The places he has showings."

She chewed on her lip, wondering if he could find Saul without her help. Patrick turned his head and considered her silence.

"Molly, you can't stop me. Why not give up this passive resistance tactic of yours?"

"Tactic? I—I didn't ask you to do battle for me," she pointed out reasonably. "It isn't your affair."

He clicked the pen in his hand absently. "You asked me not to smother you, told me to get out of your life." His eyes lifted to imprison hers. "If you want free of me, you'll speed up the process by cooperating now. Once I've got Saul to clear up the tax situation so that you've got your property back——" He shrugged and finished carelessly, "Then I'll let you go."

Let her go. The words hurt, although Molly had pinned no dreams for the future on this mission of Patrick's. She had to swallow several times before she could manage to speak. "It's not really my cabin. You have to understand Saul. He . . . well, he just doesn't think."

"He'll think next time, I promise you!" Patrick bit off a curse. "He's your father! He's supposed to love you, care for you—not dump you in this kind of trouble!"

Molly leaned forward and put her hand on his arm. Under her fingers, his muscles were rigid. "Patrick, I know he seems . . . well, uncaring, but it isn't that. It's something to do with the way he is, part of what makes him such a brilliant artist. Whatever he's looking at, that's what fills his mind and his heart. Nothing else matters. He just doesn't see consequences." Patrick's face looked even more grim as he violently snapped the pen in his fingers in half. "And he doesn't believe in taxation," she added weakly.

"I plan to teach him," said Patrick harshly. "Where is he, Molly?"

"I don't know."

Patrick stared at the broken pen. How many times had Molly had to make excuses to herself for her father? Was she lying to protect him now?

"Molly, are you going to help me?" She swallowed and he said quietly, "I'm trying to keep him out of jail, Molly."

She hugged herself, a gesture that always made him want to put his arms around her, to shelter her and love her.

"Patrick, I don't want you in this mess," she said finally. "I—I——" She knew from his face that it was no use. She sighed and closed her eyes and said quietly, "Yes. What do you want to know?"

"You don't know where he is?"

"I think he's somewhere in Europe, but I'm only guessing."

"What about your aunt?"

Molly shook her head. "He'd never tell her anything. The only thing they ever agreed about was that I should go live with Carla and her husband when I was twelve."

Patrick took Carla's telephone number anyway.

"He has a showing in Paris in September," Molly said. "He sends me invitation cards to his showings. Sometimes. Last time in Paris, it was the Sèvres gallery. How can he have got his paintings out of the country with this going on, though? Except Babette——"

"Who's Babette?"

"She came and got his paintings a couple of days after I arrived at the cabin. You remember? Saul phoned for me to pack up his paintings. You were there." Rather amazingly, Molly remembered Babette's telephone number. ''But it's just an answering service. I think she's with Saul.''

Maybe, thought Patrick, but answering machines could be accessed remotely, and Patrick thought he could lay a trap on an answering machine that would catch a vain, scatterbrained artist.

He wondered what the status of art was with the customs officials of France and Canada. He could think of ways Saul Natham could be in trouble that Molly had not even dreamed of; but he wasn't about to tell any of them to Molly. Saul Natham might not know it, but he had run his daughter's emotions ragged for the last time. It might be impossible to make a fifty-year-old man grow up, but Patrick would make damned sure that the artist would think twice and three times before he ever did anything to hurt Molly again.

For the first two days of Molly's stay at Sarah and Edward's bed and breakfast, Patrick turned up for breakfast each morning, then drove away. She assumed that he went to his offices in Nanaimo.

He came for supper each evening, eating with the family in the kitchen, not with the guests in the dining room. He seemed calmer after that first meeting in the office, more the quiet and purposeful Patrick she knew; except that there were no smiles and he avoided speaking directly to Molly—except for those nightly sessions in the office, asking questions of her, making notes on that pad.

He questioned her about the telephone numbers in Saul's address book. The book itself was sealed up in the cabin, but Patrick insisted that Molly could remember some of the numbers if she tried. Patrick himself had a mind that collected numbers and filed them accurately for future retrieval. He insisted that somewhere in Molly's mind must be stored the numbers she had dialed in her search for Saul.

"One of those numbers got through to him," Patrick insisted.

She couldn't remember the numbers, but on the third session in that office she realized that she still had the telephone bill she had paid for Saul in her bag.

She didn't realize until the next evening that Patrick must have found what he wanted among the European numbers on that telephone bill. For the first time, he didn't come to the Hollisons' for dinner.

Afterward, when the dishes were cleared away and the guests gone upstairs to their rooms, Molly slipped out into the darkness. The Hollisons' garden light took her almost to the place on the trail which Patrick's lights illuminated. His garden light was on, but his car wasn't there and the windows were dark. She wondered if his door was locked, but could not bring herself to find out. If he had locked the doors of his house, it might be a symbol of what he had done to the heart that had once loved her.

Why had she come? What had she intended to do if Patrick had been here? Go to him? Into his arms? If he felt *anything* for her, it would have to wait until the anger faded. Maybe longer, because although he had stopped breaking pens and growling at her there was no warmth anywhere.

She followed the path on from his house, but the darkness overcame the trees before she got to the cabin. Best that way, she decided. Seeing the lock on the door and the official notice there wasn't going to help anything. She had belongings inside that house, her music collection and clothes. She supposed Patrick's lawyer would spring them free, but in her heart she did not believe that even Patrick could get her cabin back. She really didn't understand why he was so determined to try. Even the lawyer had been doubtful of success. A property transfer made for the purpose of evading tax liability had to be null and void. She knew Saul wouldn't have thought of it in that cold-blooded light, but that didn't change reality or the law. Her father believed you could alter reality by believing in fairies. Where did that leave Molly, who believed in dragons and dinosaurs? And Patrick, who believed he could put any problem right?

She went back to the Hollisons' house to lie in the guest bed and listen for the sound of Patrick's car. It didn't come.

The next morning, David came into the kitchen through the back door in his work clothes. "Don't want the guests to see me," he told Molly. "They'll think this is a farm instead of a luxurious island hideaway."

He handed her two cartons of eggs and passed the message to tell Patrick to call when he returned. "I'll bring him around eggs and milk when he's back from Europe."

Europe. And she had told Patrick that Saul was probably in Europe. Had he found something from those telephone numbers?

Molly cornered Sarah in an empty guest room. Sarah was stripping the bed and Molly took the bundle of linen from her. "Where's Patrick? Where in Europe? Has he gone after Saul?"

"Yes." Sarah took the linen back. "Don't worry. It's going to be fine. Everything's going to be fine."

Molly sank down on the bed. "He's gone after Saul." She closed her eyes. "How did he find him? What did he do about Trouble?" She hadn't seen the cat yet, but Patrick had told her it came every day to his house for feeding, then ran back into the bushes.

"Jeremy's looking after feeding Trouble. As for Saul, Pat didn't tell me." Sarah's lips quirked. "He's not exactly the easiest person to talk to lately, you know."

Molly stared at Sarah's hands locked around the linen, the wide gold band digging into her finger from the grip on the sheets. "I don't understand why you're being so nice to me. As if—well, as if I were family or..."

Sarah's eyes weren't black like her brother's, but their brown depths could carry that same watchful certainty. She said, "You're family. You're the woman my brother is in love with."

Molly closed her eyes painfully. "I—I don't understand why he's doing what he's doing. I don't think I understand Patrick at all. I thought maybe I'd made him hate me, but now...I *didn't* want him messed up in all this."

"That's why you ran away, wasn't it? To protect Patrick." Sarah laughed. "Like a red flag to a bull, love."

People made sense, didn't they? If you understood why they did things, it had to make sense. Even Saul was consistent to his own weird nature. If Patrick's behavior didn't make sense, then somehow she wasn't seeing it right. Molly whispered, "Sarah, did he say why he was doing this? Did he tell you?"

"No. When you ran off, Pat abused his poor car for a few days, then started spending all his time at work." Sarah shrugged. "Typical Patrick reaction, I thought. If he'd lost you—well he doesn't give up while there's hope, but once a thing's over, he doesn't look back."

"But——" It was over. That had been the message in his voice and his eyes ever since he'd turned up outside her door in Ottawa.

Sarah put the linen down and sat beside Molly on the bed. "Then they came and padlocked your cabin. And there was that article in one of those tabloid rags, about wealthy artists who ducked out on taxes, only this artist had made a real mess of it."

Molly hadn't known about that, but it was no surprise. Saul attracted publicity even when he wasn't dodging taxes.

"Patrick stormed in here," said Sarah. "Shouting, which is a pretty unusual event, I can tell you. He said he didn't give an unprintable damn. He was blank damned if Saul Natham was going to get away with his sadistic brand of Indian giving."

"Saul's not sadistic," Molly protested weakly.

"Patrick wasn't into fine distinctions. He said if you wanted him out of your life, okay, but first he was going to straighten out one irresponsible, immature artist if it was the last thing he did."

Molly's heart was beating harder with every word. Sarah said, "Actually, the whole tirade was a lot more colorful than that." She raised expressive shoulders. "I don't envy your dad when Pat catches up with him. Anyone who treats you badly had better watch out." She covered Molly's hand with hers. "Maybe you don't realize just how amazing that is, Patrick in an emotional rage. My brother is the coolest man I've ever met. The family rock. We all turn to him, even my parents, but even when Pat's fighting for something he's always so damned rational. Cool, no matter who's involved."

Sarah got up abruptly. "Except for you." Her voice turned soft, as if she were whispering to her babies. "You, Molly, have got my brother tied in knots. I hope you plan to unravel him."

She wasn't sure if she could. He might not let her.

"Molly!" Edward shouted up from downstairs. "Will you come sign for this damned thing? The delivery man insists you've got to sign."

Her van. Sparkling and clean, parked behind the station wagon. "How did it get here?" she asked the uniformed man with the clipboard.

"Watson's delivery service."

Molly supposed you could get anything delivered if you were determined. Sarah looked more doubtful, standing in the doorway with a baby in her arms. "Patrick arranged it."

"Your furniture will come next," said Edward with an amused frown.

Molly stared at the van. She must have been in shock these last few days, perhaps ever since she ran away from the cabin.

"Furniture?" worried Sarah. "Do you think there will be furniture coming, Molly?"

"No." There wasn't any furniture, but there would be the boxes he had packed up for her in the apartment. He would have looked after their disposal and delivery. She had known that, of course, or she would have worried about her loose ends back in Ottawa. Like giving notice on the apartment, which Patrick must have settled for her.

"I'll have to teach you to stop worrying about things," he had told her a long time ago. "It's time someone looked after you."

She had screamed at him to go away, and he had gone. But then ...

"Are you going to move it?" asked Edward when the delivery man had driven away in a vehicle driven by a second uniformed man.

Molly touched her lips with her tongue.

Edward said uncomfortably, "The van, Molly. It's in my way. I've got to take the wagon to the school to pick up Jeremy and Sally."

"Okay," she said slowly. "I'll move the van." She took in a deep breath and stared at the keys. Keys. Locks. Would Patrick's front door be open? If it was locked, would he have set the bolt on the back door?

She pulled the van up beside the wagon, then sat with her fingers curled around the steering wheel. Saul, she thought grimly, you'd better listen to him. Whatever he says to you. He's doing it for me and I don't want him hurt.

She went inside and found Sarah in the family room, nursing one of the twins, the other sleeping in the bassinet beside her. Molly couldn't tell for sure if it was Tammy or Terry at Sarah's breast. She couldn't tell the babies apart when they had their diapers on.

"You should color code them," she told Sarah. "Do you know when he's coming back?"

Sarah didn't. Molly took a deep breath. "Well, I'm going to wait for him next door." She gulped and met Sarah's eyes. "If you need any help with Jeremy and Sally, could you send them over? Or phone Patrick's number? And I'll come help with the beds in the morning and—and . . . I want to be there when he gets back." She stood up abruptly.

"Good luck," Sarah said softly.

"Yeah." Molly took several deep breaths. "I said things . . . you can't just erase things you've said, can you?" She wasn't even sure what words she had screamed, only that they had been enough to send him away. Too much.

"With love," suggested Sarah, and maybe she knew, because there was certainly a lot of love in this house.

Molly hoped Patrick's door would be unlocked, and his heart. If there was no key . . . Well, she would break a window, if she had to. After everything else, surely Patrick would forgive her a window.

"Take some eggs," said Sarah. "And some milk. And you are going to take your suitcase, aren't you?" Sarah held her baby close and said thoughtfully, "Maybe you should forget the suitcase. Finding you in his shirt might just soften Pat up."

* * *

Patrick was tired. Dead tired, and probably suffering from jet lag, too. He hadn't thought, though, that he had reached the point of hallucinating.

He had flown into Vancouver International, cleared Customs and picked up his car from long term parking. Then he had driven into the West End for a marathon session with Carson. When it was all wrapped up but the details, he had left Carson to do the negotiating with Revenue Canada's lawyers and walked out to his car.

He'd wanted to get home, but he had arrived at Nanaimo too late for the last Gabriola ferry. He could have taken a hotel, but instead he had walked down to the commercial docks and managed to find a charter operator willing to make a midnight trip all the way around to Silva Bay. They had screamed along the waves in the rainy darkness. Patrick thought that the man piloting the speedboat was insane, but he had been too damned tired to care much if they hit a log. He would have given anything to be in his own bed, drifting off for eight solid hours of sleep.

For some obscure reason, the pay telephone at Silva Bay had been out of order, so Patrick had ended up walking the three miles home in the rain. Walking, dead on his feet, one foot after the other in an endless automation.

He had stumbled into his own driveway an endless time later, tempted to sink down on the grass and say to hell with it until he woke up. Just a few minutes longer, he had told himself as he plodded up the drive with his head down.

He walked right into Molly's van before he saw it. Damn! They had delivered it to the wrong place. Patrick had told them lot one, but they had brought it here and, for all he knew, Molly might not even realize it was here.

He leaned against it. He had assumed that she had her van by now, but he should have called from London to check. Except that he had not quite had the nerve to call and hear that cool voice she had been using lately. Molly, he thought, and knew the ache would not get better very soon.

"Can I stop you?" she had asked. She would have her property back soon now, but he thought she would not easily forgive him for taking over her affairs against her will. Her cabin, though, and she had loved the cabin. She might live in it once the seals were taken off. Then, given time, maybe...

How could he get from one day to the next, knowing she was a few hundred feet away, yet somehow out of his reach? Better that, he thought bleakly, than never seeing her again.

Her eyes. He had always found the love in her eyes, even before she herself had admitted it was there. Until now.

Trouble rubbed at Patrick's ankles as he opened the door to the house. He bent down, expecting a scratch and finding his stroke accepted with a purr.

"I thought you'd be next door with Molly," he said softly, closing his eyes and feeling the cat rub against him. Molly. She had transformed even this wild dose of trouble into something soft and purring. The cat had gone wild again the day she had left, but now...

"Can't rewrite history, can I?" Saul Natham had demanded of him only yesterday.

"Maybe not. But you can rewrite the future." That had been Patrick's answer. He wondered if he could make it true for himself, if he could find the love in Molly again, or if she had sealed it away too deeply for him to reach.

He shed his jacket in the living room. Someone had been here cleaning up. He was pretty sure he had left the place a mess. Sarah, he supposed, and he would have to get after her because she surely had more than enough to do these days.

He hooked his tie on the knob at the bottom of the banister and worked his buttons loose on the way up. Then he came through his bedroom door, rummaging for the light switch, and the hallucination hit, full force.

Molly was sitting up in his bed, her eyes sleepy and her curves seductively covered with one of his own T-shirts. He swallowed and blinked and she did not disappear.

She did not say a word, just stared at him with the soft question in her eyes that he had seen that first day, when she had walked into his heart. He felt dizzy, but he said carefully, "I know I'm imagining you, but I'm in no shape to deal with you. Not even in a fantasy."

"Come to bed," she said softly.

That was all he could remember in the morning. Her arms reaching out, himself stumbling toward her embrace.

He woke alone, staring at the sun beating through the window, certain that it had been a dream. Paris to London to New York to Vancouver, then that session in the lawyer's office and the crazy determination to get home the same day. No wonder he had started dreaming with his eyes open. But even now, he felt like a man who had collapsed into the arms of the one woman in the world.

He could smell her scent lingering on the pillow beside him. And, he discovered a few minutes later, there was a note downstairs on the refrigerator. He looked at the signature before the message, but it didn't say "love," just her name.

If you ever decide to wake up, I've gone next door to give Sarah a hand with odds and ends and babies.

Milk and eggs in the fridge. Molly.

He had not even kissed her. He had fallen into her arms and for all he knew, he might have started snoring before his head hit the pillow. But her van was still in the drive in front of his house, as if it belonged there.

CHAPTER ELEVEN

MOLLY had Tammy in her arms when Patrick came through the kitchen door into the Hollison family room. He stopped when he found her, his eyes asking a question. Molly felt the baby's head move against the place on her shoulder where Patrick's rough chin had burned her during the night.

Last night. He had fallen onto the bed, drawing her close in his arms, throwing one leg across hers as if to hold her close. Then she had felt the strain sag from him as he grew heavy against her. She had slept in his arms. Where she belonged.

Patrick, rubbing his cheek against her shoulder in his sleep, leaving heat on her flesh. His brand on her, and she had welcomed it with a primitive joy.

This morning his face was smooth shaven and his hair was curling, still damp. His moustache was trimmed and he had lost that exhausted look of last night. It wasn't laughter in his eyes. Not anger either.

She asked, "Did you have a good sleep?"

"I dreamed."

She flushed. She had woken tangled in his arms, his hand on her breast and her own lips against his neck. He had pulled her close when she shifted, then the tension had faded from his body again and he had dropped back into unconsciousness.

"Jet lag?" she asked now.

"Yes," he agreed. "Put the baby away, Molly."

"Away?" Her lips twitched. "In a cupboard some-where?" Her heart thudded crazily against her ribs when his eyes flashed a warning. "All right. I'm going."

He was waiting when she came back, a drink in his hand. "I found Saul," he said abruptly.

"Oh."

Patrick turned the glass in his hand. Around and around.

"In Paris?" she asked.

"London, actually. It will take a few weeks for the details to be ironed out, but your property title should be clear in the end." He shrugged. "Meanwhile, you can get access, take anything of your own out that you need. Clothes. Your tapes."

"You . . . won?"

"More or less. I don't think your father understands the principles of taxation, public goods and someone's having to pay." She nodded. Saul understood what he chose to understand. He went on, "The paintings for the showing are being assessed. Your father's signed an order to have the proceeds held in trust pending nego-tiation of a payment schedule."

"A payment schedule?" She had to laugh at that. "Saul? A schedule? What did you do to him?"

Patrick shrugged and she said, "You're not going to tell me, are you?" She moved forward and took the glass out of his hands. "What's he living on? I know him. There aren't any savings. And Patrick, I won't let you support my father."

"Stop me," he suggested.

A losing proposition, she decided, watching his eyes. "For how long?"

"Just until the Revenue Canada people settle down and allow him a reasonable portion of the proceeds— which they will when they realize they're going to get their money."

"From the paintings?"

"Yes, Molly, from the paintings. I told you he would pay his own taxes."

She chewed the inside of her cheek. "Saul can go through a terrible amount of money. He doesn't understand about money. And why should you——"

"Babette understands about money." Patrick took the glass out of her hands and set it on the coffee table. "Molly, why were you sleeping at my house? Did the paying guests push you out? I didn't think Sarah and Edward were that full right now."

"What do you mean about Babette? Do you mean she—you said she understood about money."

"Molly!" His voice was sharp. "Are Sarah and Edward full up?"

With babies, she thought wildly, but he was in no mood for jokes. "No. They're not."

She stared at his hands. They were curled in on themselves. She wished he would touch her. There had been a time when he had always reached to reassure her, and last night he had come into her arms as if it was the only place he belonged in the world.

"Molly, why were you in my bed?"

A little courage, she thought. Just a little. Easy enough to believe he cared when she was mentally adding up the clues. But now, his eyes on her, examining, not tender at all.

She sucked in a ragged breath. "I was there because I thought that if you'd brought me back here, then it had to be because you wanted me here." She rushed on, "And if you wanted me here, then that was where I belonged. At your place, not here at your sister's."

"Then why did you ever leave?"

Her hands tangled together, torturing each other. "Saul," she said. "And the tax thing all ready to explode. I—I just didn't know what to do!"

"You could have told me."

"No. You would have insisted on trying to help." She shuddered and knew that she must say this. "Patrick, remember that politician on the television that night? Here in this room? You and Edward were talking about him, and you said he should have stayed out of the public eye if he was vulnerable." She hugged herself tightly and said rigidly, "Don't you understand, Patrick? With me, you would be vulnerable to scandal. Always, because Saul won't change, and he's my father."

He was frowning and she whispered, "You've got to admit that Saul would be about the worst disaster a respectable politician could dream up."

"Molly, this political thing—it's something other people are asking of me." His frown deepened. "I'll do it if it seems right. If I think I can succeed." He touched her face fleetingly, added quietly, "And if it doesn't take anything important away from the people I care about."

She seemed to be frozen, staring at him, watching his eyes turn that bleak, grim black with no lights of laughter or love as he said, "You should have told me I was smothering you, walking all over you."

She shook her head.

His jaw tensed. "The message you screamed at me at the ferry terminal when you went away. Let go of you. Give you room to breathe. Couldn't you have told me? Before it turned into an explosion? We could have worked it out."

"They were just words," she whispered. "Any words. I was desperate to get away before I dumped all Saul's tangles on to you. I—I don't even know what I said."

"I can't buy that, Molly. Those words came from somewhere. Maybe you wouldn't have chosen to say them otherwise, but they were there in your mind." She saw his fingers clench and he finished quietly but grimly, "I'll give you whatever space you need. You said I smothered you. That you needed room to breathe. I'll give you room.''

''Patrick—you're telling me you'll let me handle my own problems? The way you let me handle this tax thing?''

His control snapped. ''Molly—— Hell!'' He cut himself short and spun away from her to the window, glaring at an innocent dogwood tree.

Behind Molly, a door opened and Edward's voice called out cheerfully, ''Pat! There you are! Listen, David saw your car down at the terminal on the Nanaimo side. Did you want——?''

''Get the hell out of here!'' Patrick spun around, glowering at Edward.

Abruptly, the door closed. Molly whispered, ''Darling, it's his house.''

He stared at her, then she saw the tension slowly drain from his body. ''Did you call me *darling*?'' She nodded and her eyes turned from blue to green. Patrick saw all the words of love that she had never felt free to give him until now.

''Are you sure, Molly? If you're here, near me, I can wait. You've got to be sure.''

She touched his arm. ''My darling Patrick, I've always loved you.''

He reached for her and she said on a breathless rush, ''Please will you start looking after me again? If you overdo it, I promise I'll say. I—please——'' She laughed breathlessly. ''Say something! Do something! I don't know how to finish this scene. I—do you still love me?''

He closed his eyes briefly and marvelled in a shaken voice, ''I don't believe you asked that. There can't be anyone between here and London who doesn't know what I feel about you.''

She knew, had always known in her heart. She touched his chest fleetingly, felt the shudder of reaction go through him. He moved to her, his eyes shifting from warmth to fire.

"You should know better than anyone," he said wryly. "I used to have an even temper. The only person I'd ever shouted at was my older brother, and that was years back." He took her face in his hands gently. "Molly, darling, you're the only person in the world who can destroy me by walking away. I never knew anyone could have that kind of power over me, never wanted it...until I saw you. You're...light and color and love. Everything."

Her lips moved toward his and he brushed them tenderly, "So much more than passion, Molly. You're so deep in me, I can feel every breath you take. I want to look after you, slay your dragons and protect you." He cleared his throat and admitted, "I don't seem to be able to stop myself needing to do that for you. All I can promise is that I'll try not to do it more than you want. I—oh, God, Molly! Don't cry!"

"Then do something about it," she whispered. "Take me home. Protect me from the bears."

He laughed low in his throat. "There aren't any bears."

She knew better. Her love had already slain the bears, not to mention the dragons. He took her hand and led her toward the back door. She worried. "Shouldn't we say something to Sarah and Edward? You shouted at him."

"Yes, we should," he agreed. "But we won't. They'll forgive us. Sarah will even come help you when we have our children." He pushed her through the door, closed them both outside.

"I left my purse inside. And my jacket. And..." She was trembling deep inside, but although she said, "It's cold out here," she could feel the warm excitement growing. *Our* children.

He drew her close. "I'll keep you warm." He knew the way and she followed, a smile on her lips and a song in her heart.

"You realize," she warned him, "you have to marry me if you really mean it about the children."

He stopped walking and took her fully into his arms. It was a long time before she could breathe, much less talk. Then she gasped, "Has it occurred to you that whatever it is that makes a Saul Natham might be genetic? That you're taking a risk?"

"Whatever it is that makes the woman I love might be genetic, too. And besides, you and I could tame even Saul Natham."

He drew her toward his house, but she held back, insisting, "He'll do other things. One day he'll do something that will splash your name all over the media with his."

"Maybe," he agreed easily. "Don't you understand yet, darling? First in my life, before anything else, comes the woman I love."

She let him draw her up the stairs. "You mean, I'm not to worry?"

"You're learning, my love." He opened the unlocked front door and swung her up into his arms. "Welcome home, Molly," he whispered, and carried her inside.

HARLEQUIN PRESENTS®

BARBARY WHARF

Home to the *Sentinel*
Home to passion, heartache and love

Charlotte Lamb

The BARBARY WHARF six-book saga concludes with Book Six, SURRENDER. The turbulent relationship between Nick Caspian and Gina Tyrrell reaches its final crisis. Nick is behaving like a man possessed, and he claims Gina's responsible. She may have declared war on him, but one thing is certain— Nick has never surrendered to anyone in his life and he's not about to start now. Will this final battle bring Nick and Gina together, or will it completely tear them apart?

SURRENDER (Harlequin Presents #1540)
available in March.

HARLEQUIN ✦ PRESENTS®

A Year
DOWN UNDER

In 1993, Harlequin Presents celebrates the land down
under. In March, let us take you to Northland, New
Zealand, in THE GOLDEN MASK by Robyn Donald,
Harlequin Presents #1537.

Eden has convinced herself that Blade Hammond won't
give her a second look. The grueling demands of trying to
keep the sheep station running have left her neither the
money nor the time to spend on pampering herself.
Besides, Blade still considers her a child who needs
protecting. Can Eden show him that she's really a woman
who needs his love . . . ?

Share the adventure—and the romance—
of A Year Down Under!

Available this month in
A YEAR DOWN UNDER

NO GENTLE SEDUCTION
by Helen Bianchin
Harlequin Presents #1527
Wherever Harlequin books are sold.

YDUF

Take 4 bestselling love stories FREE

Plus get a FREE surprise gift!

Where do you find hot Texas nights, smooth Texas charm and dangerously sexy cowboys?

DEEP IN THE HEART

Wedding Bells—Texas Style!

Even a Boston blue blood needs a Texas education. Ranch owner J. T. McKinney is handsome, strong, opinionated and totally charming. And he is determined to marry beautiful Bostonian Cynthia Page. However, the couple soon discovers a Texas cattleman's idea of marriage differs greatly from a New England career woman's!

CRYSTAL CREEK reverberates with the exciting rhythm of Texas. Each story features the rugged individuals who live and love in the Lone Star State. And each one ends with the same invitation...

Y'ALL COME BACK...REAL SOON!

Don't miss *DEEP IN THE HEART* by Barbara Kaye. Available in March wherever Harlequin books are sold.

CC-1

ROMANCE IS A YEARLONG EVENT!

Celebrate the most romantic day of the year with MY VALENTINE! (February)

CRYSTAL CREEK
When you come for a visit Texas-style, you won't want to leave! (March)

Celebrate the joy, excitement and adjustment that comes with being JUST MARRIED! (April)

Go back in time and discover the West as it was meant to be . . . UNTAMED— Maverick Hearts! (July)

LINGERING SHADOWS
New York Times bestselling author Penny Jordan brings you her latest blockbuster. Don't miss it! (August)

BACK BY POPULAR DEMAND!!!
Calloway Corners, involving stories of four sisters coping with family, business and romance! (September)

FRIENDS, FAMILIES, LOVERS
Join us for these heartwarming love stories that evoke memories of family and friends. (October)

Capture the magic and romance of Christmas past with HARLEQUIN HISTORICAL CHRISTMAS STORIES! (November)

WATCH FOR FURTHER DETAILS IN ALL HARLEQUIN BOOKS!

CALEND